My Head Upon the 10-Pound Note

Time-Travel Jane

Bonus:

PERSUASION CHARACTERS SPEAK OUT
or *'The Elliot Pride'*

Mary Flannery

DEDICATION

To writers and artists who, though long gone to
'that undiscover'd country from whose bourne no traveller returns'
still give us respite and joy in the works they left after them.

And to Limerick, Clare and the Shannon Region, rich in
Natural Beauty, History, Heritage and Culture.

CONTENTS

ACKNOWLEDGMENTS

Thanks to Deirdre Le Faye for her book 'Jane Austen's Letters'; to Claire Tomalin for her Biography 'Jane Austen – A Life'; to Paula Byrne for 'The Real Jane Austen, A Life in Small Things'; to Maggie Lane for the book 'Jane Austen's World'; to William Laffan's fine book 'Painting Ireland' for his description of the Limerick Assembly Rooms; to Valerie Pakenham's 'the Big House in Ireland' from which I learned of the incident of the Abduction Club; the numerous online Resources especially Linda Robinson Walker's 'Persuasions on-line' JASNA article on 'Jane Austen and Tom Lefroy'; Laurel Ann Nattress' Austenprose; Vic Sanborn's Jane Austen's World and other Austen websites and to the Gutenberg Project for 'The Life and Letters of Maria Edgeworth'; and humbly, to Wikipedia for jump-starting my searches – you are always up first, Wiki, in a Google search, eagerness itself to help...

To Liam for his support of my numerous writing projects, and to my parents, siblings and relatives for their interest and encouragement.

My Head Upon the 10-Pound Note

Time-Travel Jane

Introduction

Cassandra was Jane Austen's sister, older by three years. Whenever they were apart, they wrote to each other constantly. Jane sometimes made references to her fictional characters in her letters to Cassandra.

To avoid cluttering the text with footnotes, (I found it necessary to include some, usually in relation to other Nineteenth-Century Authors) it is simpler to name her brothers here. They were James, a clergyman; Edward, a wealthy landowner upon whom Jane, her widowed mother and Cassandra financially depended; Frank and Charles, Naval Officers; Henry, a Banker, the brother closest to Jane, who in 1816 had become bankrupt. Another brother, George, ten years older than Jane, was mentally handicapped and lived away from home. Any mention, if any, of George in Jane's correspondence has not survived.

Martha Lloyd, a close friend, lived with the Austen women at Chawton Cottage. Cassandra and Jane had numerous nieces and nephews and were devoted aunts. The Austens were also very close to their cousin, Eliza de Feuillide. Born in India, as a young girl she captivated her cousins while on long visits to them, charming them with her vivacious personality and bringing to them the world outside Steventon. She married a French nobleman who was guillotined, and afterwards married Henry Austen. She died in 1813.

This novella was mainly inspired by the thought - how is it that the work of this early nineteenth-century author, who wrote of country families and country manners, has captured the affections of our frantic, high-tech world? Would this surprise Miss Austen? The writer could not resist planning a little trip for her favourite author across Time to 2016, to the city of Limerick, Ireland, which was also the birthplace of Jane's amour Tom Lefroy.

.

Dear Cassandra

What a surprise it will be for you to receive a letter from me, since you and I bid each other goodnight last night, and you blew out the candle and then we settled down in our beds to sleep until morning.

Or so you thought. If you wake up during the night, and see a lump in my bed, it will not be me at all, but a 3D copy of Jane.

Do not ask me what that means; for I do not really know myself. I am gone for the night, to the Future; am seated in a very cozy armchair, though strapped in - I have borrowed a Pen, which produces Ink by itself, and a sheet of thin paper, which I hope you will excuse. Here is how it all came about:

As I was falling asleep I felt myself drift into that strange path that connects waking and sleeping, a path of sometimes odd sights and sensation. I was in a bright, airy room, and there was met by a spectacle indeed – I shall attempt to describe it – a young woman with dark eyes and shiny black hair in spiral curls to her shoulders, dressed in a theatrical costume - a tight black bodice with long sleeves, a short black petticoat with a purple zig-zag pattern, and black hose. Her jewellery shimmered silver and amethyst. The girl's eyelids and browbone were amethyst and ashy colours, her lips stained purply-red. She appeared to have been waiting for me, and smiled warmly, showing very good teeth.

By this creature's side was a thin table made of silvery metal, and

11

upon this lay a shallow box, of a darker silver, and the hinged lid of which was open. The inside of this lid was illuminated by flashing lines in all colours – faster than the eye could follow! My eyes fixed upon this show, fascinated by the lights and marvelling at the trick, when the young woman addressed me, and speaking rapidly, so that her words tripped over each other, began with words that sounded thus:

'Oh, Miss Oasten! Welcome! My name is Gina, eand I represent Time Travel Tours, oah TTT for showat. We are a Company based in Nee Yuorhk with affiliates in several cities and countries. I'm from the year 2016. Miss Oasten, you've heard of the Space Time Continuum?'

I had not, but anything is possible in a dream, I suppose – 'I have *heard* of it now', I heard myself say. 'Please explain, but speak more slowly. I am having the greatest difficulty understanding you.'

'Oh, I'm sorry, Miss Oasten. It's my accent. I will try to do bedda. *Better*. The Space Time Continuum is very complicated. I don't understand it myself, and I majored in Graphics Communications, not Science. But the juob market is tight, and this was the only juob I could get eaftah – *aftah* -Graduation.'

'I see. Pray go on, Miss Gina.' By now I had forgotten I was in a Dream, and was taking everything with a lack of surprise.

'It's just Gina, Miss Oasten. We offah our Clients a unique experience; a trip to another Time and Place. Miss Oasten, we can get you on our *British Litehachew 19th Century Tour* without delay; and as our Guest we eask only that you do some promotional work for us, in allowing your experience to be requowded – *recorded* - by us for the purpose of promoting Time Travel Tours.'

I deciphered what she said, all the time highly diverted by her accent. I have never heard anybody speak like that before, and to spare you having to decipher it yourself, I will now switch from the phonetic spelling of her words to that which you are familiar with, for I *was* beginning to understand her, and I shall never finish the letter if I have to '*requowd*' it in her dialect. But imagine it, if you can – short vowels, o before a. Forgetting 'r' now and then. A little nasal as well, but not unattractive; it rather suits her overall pert appearance.

'Miss Austen, this is the experience of a lifetime, and I am sure one you would not want to miss. It is Free. Nothing to pay; nothing to lose – risk-free, and it can all be done in one night while you sleep. What do you say?'

'It sounds a very attractive prospect indeed!'

'That means - yes?' She smiled, and her eyes sparkled, as she said with excitement, as if I had just bestowed a gift of ten guineas upon her: 'Oh thank you, Miss Austen! I'm going to meet my quota. I have to book eighty per month. Not all to *Brit Lit* of course…this is a small tour, only five or six people.'

BritLit. Indeed! The abbreviation both amused and irritated me. Have the Americans snipped English to pieces?

She turned suddenly and tapped the surface of the silvery box on the table. The lights stopped dancing on the inside lid, and were replaced by a column of words and vivid paintings. I could see a Heading – TTT with a symbol of a Flying Kite. I drew closer. The lid was lit up as if it were a clear pool on a summers day. I became aware of a hum that I had been hearing ever since I entered this room, a continuous low hum.

I was mistaken that this metal object was a box, however – the 'inside' was no hollow, but had shiny metal letters each on it's own little block, and numbers and symbols. Gina was tapping upon these with long bright red nails at incredible speed, and as she tapped the letters on the lid changed rapidly to form full words; pictures flashed on and off in the blink of an eye.

'That is an amazing Show!' I said with astonishment.

'What is it?'

'Oh, this? It's a computer – a laptop.'

'But what is it's purpose?'

'Oh, it's for Writing. Data Entry, Word Processing, Spreadsheets, all that.'

'It is a writing desk!'

'A writing desk?' She looked amused.

'I have a writing desk that my father gave me many years ago. It has a sloping lid, and I set it on my lap when I am travelling if I wish to review my writing. It is a good way to pass a journey, though difficult to use the pen and ink because of the swaying.'

'And this is – in a horse-drawn carriage?'

'Yes, how else? It was left in a carriage once, and could have ended up in the West Indies, but we found out on time and sent a man after it. That is, on a horse.'

'Oh it is really easy to lose laptops and notebooks,' she said with seriousness. 'And then they steal all your files – uh, work.'

'Quite so', I said smilingly, '*Pride and Prejudice* may have narrowly escaped coming out in Jamaica.'

Gina looked a little blank, and I supposed she has not heard of P&P? I felt just a little sad that it is probably out of print in 2016, and may have been for quite some time.

'You –have not heard of - *Jamaica*?' I ventured, courage failing me. It is over two hundred years, after all! Who could hope to be remembered? And yet I have been marked down for this *British Literature 'Tour'*…

'Miss Austen! Of course I have heard of Jamaica! And I have heard of *Pride and Prejudice*! I saw the movie! Keira Knightley. I loved the scene where he comes out of the mist – Dawn is so very romantic.'

Knightley? - My hero from *Emma*, but nobody comes out of a mist in P&P…I am all at sea.

'I'm seeing if I can get you on the Tour. There – the 19th Century British Literature Tour. *BritLit19th* for short.'

'Where am I going?'

'Limerick, Ireland. Early Twenty-First Century.' Gina tapped again.

'Limerick!' I exclaimed. My heart lurched in my chest! But does he still have that kind of power over me, when the mention of his home city affects me so? Should I go?

'Limerick, Ireland, 2016.' Gina said, looking up at me with expectation before turning her eyes to the laptop. 'It's a city with a really nice Georgian section, and our Cultural Interpreter chose it for that. It has castles and luxury hotels and pubs. It boasts a fine University in a setting of natural beauty and it's close to Shannon Airport. ' She seemed to be reading from the inside lid.

15

My silence is consent - she tapped again, twice.

'There, it's a Go. I just need to get your Dimensions.'

'My what?'

'Dimensions. We need to make a 3D copy of you - a hi-tech model - that will take your place in your bed. Could you just step into this frame?'

She indicated a silver door frame standing upright by itself upon a mat. I did as I was bid. A round red flame blazed in a panel upon the wall directly in front of me.

'Face that light in front of you - hold still – hold your breath! Now close your eyes! Close your eyes, Miss Austen! Look peaceful!' – a Noise like *ClickClickWhoooshClick*! - ' There! You can come out now.'

I stepped out. Tap, tap tap again with her long fingernails, and I began to hear other sounds, loud scratching noises, like a roomful of scribes busy with their Quills. It came from another room.

'It's only the Printer.'

I imagined a gruff man with inky apron, ill-humoured from cleaning the plates, but decided that my image must be incorrect.

'It will take a few minutes'. Gina examined her scarlet nails and shook her head. 'Twenty dollars for a manicure and it's chipping. I am never going to *Glam-Glam Nails* again. Do you think I should complain?'

'I cannot counsel you upon that point,' I say faintly, my ears upon the scratch, scratch sound. 'Having never been to one of those establishments, indeed, having never painted my nails.'

'Oh,' Gina said. 'Of course. I forgot. It's a modern thing.' There was silence except for the scratching sound. An occasional pause, and then it went more slowly and suddenly ceased.

Gina got up from her chair and darted into the next room, and I gasped when she returned, for she was pushing a little cart on wheels, and upon the cart lay a figure in a long white nightgown and nightcap, eyes closed in peaceful slumber. It looked very like me.

Gina smiled brightly.

That's a 3D copy of you,' she said. She turned the figure upon it's side, and began to quickly arrange the arms, tucking one hand under the cheek, and bent the knees slightly. Drawing near, I saw that the figure was made of some kind of plaister. I even had fingernails!

'Do I have a brain?' I asked, smiling.

'No,' she giggled. 'but it can be programmed to say certain things like if someone tells you to get up, it can say: 'Leave me alone,' or 'Go away.' But this software – *DuplicYou* - is not perfect. It's a rip-off of *RealBod*, which is the Industry Standard. But Time Travel Tours are too cheap to lay out the funds for *RealBod*. You see, it doesn't do noses that really well, yours might be a bit short.'

I peered at my face with keenness; it was true.

She went to the laptop again, tap, tap, and my chest began to move gently up and down.

'*DuplicYou*'s breathing sounds so artificial, we never turn up the volume. But as long as people can see you breathe, it should be OK. And it's programmed to turn you every four hours. *Realbod* can do it every two hours. That is probably more realistic.'

17

'You should invest in *RealBod*.' I say with grave countenance.

'My thoughts exactly. OK, Jane! I don't have to keep calling you Miss Austen, do I? Nobody does that nowadays. What do you think of yourself?' The copy of me, in my nightgown and bare feet, lay curled in peaceful sleep. 'You have really gorgeous sleepwear,' Gina continued. 'It's so quaint. All those little satin-covered buttons! The little cap is so cute! Ruffles and ribbons! Did you make everything yourself?'

'I sewed every stitch,' I said, gratified. Not everybody can see anything to admire in a plain old nightgown and cap, though the cap is Irish linen.

Cassandra, I do not know if I shall remember this dream to tell you but if I do, it will divert us greatly at breakfast. I will try to remember at least '*Miss Oasten.*' OK Cass!

Your Affectionate Sister

Jane

September 19th 2016 - later

My Dear Cassandra

I had hardly time to ask any questions, when Gina wished me a good journey, and left. I was at a loss and wished I had not been so hasty. She took with her the model of myself, and I suppose that as I write it lies in my bed, breathing in and out though my shortened nose, without a sound.

I was contemplating the ugliness of a windowless room when the door opened again and a blonde-haired woman walked briskly in.

18

She too wore cosmetics, though favoured a more muted look than Gina, her eyelids being only a greyish brown. She was clothed in what looked like a lady's riding jacket, only shorter and simpler - a piece of bright canary lace was visible at her throat, and a slim, very narrow petticoat reached her knees. Both garments went together in their grey colour and smart style, and it struck me that the petticoat has become outside wear. What a great saving on gowns! She was *bare legged*, and her grey shoes were flat upon the ground, and looked incredibly dull. Her hair was almost as yellow as her lace, and stiff with a colourless pomade, for it was immobile. I hope you can picture her as I did, and add a quivering sort of energy.

'Good evening, Jane – I may call you that? I'm Rena, and I'm Director of the European Affiliate of Time Travel Tours. I'm so happy you have joined us! ' She held her hand out quickly to shake mine, catching me off-balance as I made a curtsey, for this was a person of higher rank than Gina. She spoke like her, but with a pronunciation that was easier on my ears. The handshake was an intimacy that surprised me, but then everything was different.

She bid me go through a door, where I saw a pile of what were some of my own cloathes, and my boots alongside. She bid me change, and after that sat me into an armchair, and secured me with a belt. At that point I asked for the writing materials, which she was happy to provide, and I wrote the first letter, with the paper steadied upon a large book called *'Martha's Vineyard in Color'* which I found on a table by my side. Rena then stuck a needle in my arm – did you ever hear of such a thing? It was only the size of the smallest in my huswife[1], and was connected to a small tube in which I perfectly beheld a *liquid*. The needle hardly

---

[1] needlecase

19

hurt, and I must have been put to sleep - and when I opened my eyes, I was in a different place - walking down a long shining hallway, with a row of windows looking out upon a cluster of high buildings, and down an immense way upon a great city, a blue sea beyond, and out on the water, a large green statue of a woman with a crown and upraised arm. I thought I was looking from Heaven. Was I in the Afterlife?

'Orientation begins in just two minutes,' Rena said, hurriedly, as she ushered me away from the view and down a hallway to our right, still full of light in spite of there being no windows or candles. 'There will be quite a motley crew there; all from different places and times – Sir! Sir! No weapons allowed in the building!'

The dark bearded man she addressed had a noble mien, he wore flowing medieval cloathes of fine stuff, and had a rather cross countenance, and he looked at her with disdain as she pointed at a sign on the wall. He put his hand protectively to the bejeweled sword by his side.

'I wish we didn't have to take pre-Renaissance,' she grumbled. 'That, by the way, is King John. He wants to go on *BritLit19th*. Doug!' She inclined her head towards a young man shadowing the King. 'Why did you not persuade him to join *Medieval Military*? I would have thought that he would be very happy.'

King John's attendant cut a good figure, possessed a fine countenance, and was dressed in what I assumed was today's cloathes for men - long well-cut trousers, a well-fitted shirt in a subtle check pattern. It was tucked in at the waist, and had narrow sleeves with neat cuffs. Smart and sensible.

'I'm still working on it, Rena,' he said smilingly. 'He's afraid some dude he hated from France was going to be on it. Hugh Something. '

'There is no Hugh on *Medieval Military*,' said Rena. 'I know, because I checked the Guest Database on my way here.'

Doug explained to the King, who was still resistant, until he told him he would not be safe in Limerick, as the O'Briens were in firm possession of the City, and were said to be invincible. This did the trick, and Doug looked over at me, whose countenance showed my amusement, and he said in a low tone: 'It pays to use the imagination a little – after doing the research of course.' – by which I deduced that the O'Briens were not in charge of Limerick.

'Good for you, Doug,' Rena said warmly.

We had halted at a set of double doors leading to a large Hall. Doug picked up something from a table.

'Your Majesty, here's your card –color-code blue.'

'Why do I haf to wear a sign, like a thief in the stocks? ' asked the King.

'You have to wear your Name Tag or nobody will know who you are or when you came from. It will ensure respect for your noble station. It's just pinned to your – tunic.'

He consented and walked on.

'You're welcome!' Doug said as the King entered the Hall, without as much as a backward glance. 'No thanks, no tip. Nothing. He has to have a few gold pieces in his pocket. Hey, Your Majesty! Come back! You get a Pen and a Snickers Bar as well!'

21

The aforementioned items were upon the table. I was presented with one of each, and I received my card also, coloured green:

BRITISH LITERATURE 19TH CENT
JANE AUSTEN
1816

After which I proceeded into the Hall, a high cavernous room without beauty or decoration. Again, there was not one window, but bright lights emanated from panels in the ceiling. It was bare of furniture except for a few tables set with food and punch-bowls, a number of ill-favoured chairs scattered about, and nothing upon the pale walls except a large white banner with *Welcome to Time Travel Tours* above a platform. An invisible Orchestra played tinkling music. There was a considerable crowd before me, milling about, helping themselves to punch, or talking in groups.

'Where in the world are we?' I asked Rena. 'We are not in England, I think.'

'Not anymore. Orientation always takes place in our H.Q in New York. It's more cost-effective to bring everyone over here than have multiple sessions in several different countries. The bean counters copped that one.'

'The City, outside – we are very high up, are we not?'

'We're on the 77th Floor.'

I exclaimed in surprise, and wished to ask her how so many stairs were to be managed, but she bustled me into the Hall, and left. I will write more a little later, but I wish to get at the punch, for I am very thirsty.   Your affect. Sister, Jane

My Dear Cassandra,

I miss you very much and wish you could be here with me. No doubt you miss me too - I shall be insulted if you say otherwise, and sleeping is no excuse.

I do not know if my letters will reach you or not – it does not signify. Every time we are apart we write, and so I write, as it is as natural as breathing when we are apart. So I shall set down all I see, and write as usual.

I was only meant to be away for seven hours, and in Chawton-time that is what it is, but I have just found out that in the Space Time Continuum it is possible for me to spend days and nights here within those seven hours. Gina was supposed to inform me of that, but I suppose she forgot. Rena told me she has *Boyfriend Trouble.* Oh, and she was not in costume. I have seen plenty of tight bodices, short skirts and hose since I arrived here – some of the hose is footless and ends above the ankles.

But to return to my story – the said *Orientation*. The people in the Hall had an astonishing array of garb. Old styles I knew well from illustrations and portraits. Some shocking attire in these times for ladies – a great deal of leg showing, and tight trousers which outline the figure. If I did not know better I would think some had appeared today in their underwear. None of these women wore hats or gloves, and many had short haircuts, and everybody wore cosmetics.

But some fashions resembled ours in one way or another, and their wearers must have been closer to us in Time. I spied two women standing awkwardly by the wall, they looked like sisters, and wore high-necked gowns narrow at the waist, with long hooped skirts; sleeves wider at the cuff than at the elbow, with linen undersleeves. Their hair was parted in the middle and drawn back tightly under bonnets. They had the look of clergymen's daughters, and who should know that, if not I? The older one was small and plain and looked around her with interest, as if she would have liked to have made the acquaintance of all present, but did not know where to begin; the taller, younger, more beautiful one was bone-thin, with a fierce look. I was too far away to see their names.

A group of Restoration gentlemen were examining their Pens. They were excited as puppies; and must have Paper, it seems, or die. I congratulated myself for having secured some for myself earlier, and since Rena never asked me for the pen back, I now have Two. One has to look to everything important. I did not however, succeed in bringing *Martha's Vineyard in Color* with me, so I am deprived of seeing Martha tend her plants.

Making my way down the Hall, trying to find a purpose, I was very happy to see, in a corner, a woman in middle age who was dressed in almost the same style of fashion as myself, only a great deal more expensively, with a fur tippet and gold bracelets. She was of a very short stature, but bore herself as a lady of rank. She was busy investigating the Snickers Bar, holding it in one hand, worrying it with the other. Nobody was going to introduce anybody in this company, so I drew near with the intention of making myself seen. She noticed me, and evidently saw no need for formality either, and to my relief began a conversation, as her higher rank made me uneasy about speaking first. Without any preamble, she said:

'It is a packet, you see, open it at the end – there – and what have we? A confection! Excuse my deplorable manners, but I am about to bite into it, for I am very hungry indeed - '

Her accent had a slight brogue; and her easy manners betrayed her origins - Irish! My heart leaped when I saw her name-tag - she is *Maria Edgeworth!* She too has joined *BritLit 19th*, and had come from 1816 also.

Maria Edgeworth! The famous authoress, whose works are found in every home with a bookcase, and with whom the Austens have spent many a long winter evening, with *'Belinda'*, *'Leonora'* and more recently *'Patronage'* and her many engaging stories. My muse, and along with Lennox, Smith and Burney, my female inspirers! How many times have I read aloud to you, and our mother – and our father too, when he was alive – from Maria Edgeworth! Remember I sent her a copy of my *Emma* when it came out. Becoming well-known myself, I had the assurance to send her one of my works. I could hardly believe I was meeting her in person!

'Miss Edgeworth!' I exclaimed. 'I am happy to make your acquaintance! How strange we should meet upon this journey. Permit me to introduce myself – I am Miss Jane Austen.'

She looked up from the Snickers Bar in pleased surprise, and returned my curtsey with a gracious one of hers. Her eyes were very penetrating, and very blue.

'How delightful, Miss Austen! A fellow-author! I had hoped to meet many upon this Tour. You were so good as to send me – *Emma*. A well-told story.' (this said, I thought, with a little condescension – but she speaks from a superior position in her success) 'I pray, do you know who those two females are?' - inclining her head toward me with a conspiratorial air, and nodding toward the sisters, while taking a bite from her Snickers.

I replied in the negative, realizing at the same time that she does not seem as enchanted to meet me as I her, (though I have met with recognition in England by now after four published novels) and seemed very ready to become distracted by her Snickers and the curious ladies.

'We should go over and introduce ourselves, for I do not think they will come over here,' Miss Edgeworth said. 'and as they have green cards like ours, we may be on the same Tour. If they are Authors, I wish to know. This is very interesting. Nougat. (takes a bite) Caramel. (bites again) Nuts and Chocolate. Where is yours? You should try it, as I have done. It all appears to be very *laissez-faire* hereabouts, and nobody would mind, I am sure, if one stood upon one's head.'

'Yes, I am sure you are right,' I replied. 'I have enjoyed your novels,' I added, unready to leave the subject of her work, hoping I was mistaken in her air to me. We must have so much to talk of!

'Oh, yes, how nice of you to read them! But – I am not sure if I would call them novels, you know!'

I was a little surprised; for novels are considered by some to be below other works, and I asked her: 'and what would you call your works, Miss Edgeworth?'

She looked a little uncomfortable, I thought.

'They are moral tales, Miss Austen. For education. If they entertain in the process, that is a desirable thing, but not their chief object.'

'I am of the opinion that the novel can teach, also' I said boldly. 'I have a novel, which explores that very subject, but it is not yet published.'

'A novel exploring the novel. I look forward to reading it,' Miss Edgeworth said with an interest that appeared to be genuine. 'It is to be published soon, then?'

'The date is uncertain,' I said to her. I did not tell her it's sad history; that after ten long years, I had to buy it back from Crosby, and it is now gathering dust, and I do not know if my work about Miss Moreland and Northanger Abbey will ever see print. I did not tell her that I use her Name in my argument for the Novel!

We paused in our conversation, to take in the view of two women walk past us. Their faces were painted, their hair coloured an unnatural gold, and their garments mostly black.

'They are most certainly not Nuns,' Maria mused in a whisper. 'And they cannot be in mourning, for there is a great deal of black about, and half of this room cannot have lost a relative. It must be fashionable to wear black; how practical!'

I nodded, but my mind was distracted. I do not know if Maria Edgeworth likes my work, and it occurs to me that she may look down upon it. Cassandra, I feel not a little disappointed. I have shown her my Darling Children and she has not admired them as they should be admired! After I have praised hers! I felt deflated for a few minutes, and found myself not wishing to talk more. But there was no necessity for more conversation; we were all of us assaulted by a dreadful loud noise, a shrill horn that crescendoed to fill the entire Hall, which caused everyone to gasp, startle, and look about for the source. The younger sister across the room pressed her hands to her ears, and screamed. I will go on with this later –

Dear Cass,

I am sitting on a comfortable chair at the end of a lobby, and this time my paper rests upon 'Futures'. And this has nothing to do with Time Travel. Apparently one can get very rich from reading this publication.

This is a hall with several doorways, but they do not lead to rooms, rather to closets (small ones, very small) that move up and down to convey people between the storeys of this high building. Every moment, a bell signals the arrival of one of these, and the door opens and a stream of smart people emerge and walk briskly by to the hallways leading off the lobby. Standing by the doors for the arrivals, are those waiting to get in. I do not know how it all works; the people demonstrate no anxiety, but I would not like to be shut up in a closet moving up and down between the walls.

The dreadful noise I mentioned turned out to be a fault in the 'sound system' a term understood by few females wearing hemlines past the knee, and seemed like no surprise to the rest. The men had varied reactions. The Restoration group shouted 'Murder!' but I think they were rather enjoying it all.

In any case, this noise was apologized for profusely by Rena, who had mounted the stage, and delivered a Welcome, and then explained the Rules while Doug ran through the crowd, bestowing upon everybody a small bag, blue for men, pink for women. It is of a shiny material. And this is what it is important to remember in 2016 –

Rank is of no Consequence.
Our Persons smelling sweet is of the most Consequence. To this end, we are encouraged to Bathe daily. Rena waved a short sticklike object, one of which was to be found in everybody's bag, please read the instructions on how to use it. The result of not

doing this is *Certain Societal Demise.* We were also strongly encouraged to Clean our Teeth, and those going to America should consider using the Whitener provided.

There are no personal Servants. We are our own Servants.

We are discouraged from visiting Bookshops. If we come by anything written about ourselves which occurs after the Year we have come from, we read them at our own risk.

All of our memories of this Trip (and any information gained) will be wiped out before we are taken home. Threads may remain, as threads in a dream.

Guests who know and reveal future bad events in another's life will be subject to a Disciplinary Committee. (I assume they are taken to Europe in the height of the Plague).

We will find in our Bags a Book of Instructions explaining Modern Plumbing. We are to Please read it Now.

We will be expected to sign a Contract which allows Time Travel Tours to use us for Promotion, and a waiver releasing Time Travel Tours from any Liability for anything lost, stolen, or for any harm incurred to our persons or possessions.

After we signed the Contract, we formed a queue to have our Likenesses taken. We were to accomplish that before changing into our Time-Appropriate Clothing and we were to depart for our Destinations within the hour.

This caused a stir, unless they have a team of very quick artists. It turned out to be accomplished by Doug and others at Laptops, and all we had to do was sit ten seconds in front of a screen depicting a tropical scene with golden sands, green palms and a blue sea. We were instructed to smile, and they decided to leave Miss Emily Brontë (the younger sister) out of it, for she refused to smile and they said that she could not be used on 'any promo'.

The painting was like one I had seen of the West Indies, and

29

curious, I asked Doug why we were to sit before it.

'It's not doing it for me either, but it was all we had,' he replied. 'TTT is on a tight budget, this is a leftover from the last company Rena ran, some Real Life tourist thing. Anyway, Palm Trees *sell*.'

'Where is Gina?' I asked.

'She took a few hours off to see her mom in Queens. That's a borough of New York. She's actually Company Rep/Tour Guide for *BritLit19th*,' he said. 'So she'll be accompanying you.'

'That will our pleasure,' I said, for though Gina dresses like a medieval page, and her face and eyes look like an artist's palette, she emanates warmth and friendliness. Doug too was a pleasant young man, helpful, pleasant and courteous, and I spent a while wondering if he was a Henry Tilney or a Charles Bingley.

'Oh, Miss Austen,' he said to me in a low voice. 'You seem like a nice lady, and I wonder if I could ask a favour of you. It's kind of personal, but it's very important, and would mean a lot to me.'

I am very curious, and agreed without delay. After all, Mr. Tilney or Mr. Bingley would never ask anything untoward.

'It's about Gina,' he said quietly while the laptop was going through its maneuvers. 'We were an item, um - dating, you know – 'attached' I think you say - and she heard a rumour about me – a rumour that wasn't true. She left me. I think about her all the time and I want her back, but she won't even speak to me, return my calls, anything.'

'You are in love with Gina?'

'Yes. You see, it's complicated. Before I met her she was seeing a guy named Rowland Hatton. He's a jerk. But I think she still thinks about him. But he is – how shall I say it in your Terminology – Early Modern English – he is *not worthy of* Gina.'

'Very well expressed indeed!'

'Gina doesn't have any – ok what is the word – *Fortune*. Rowland wants to marry Money. He is in debt up to his eyeballs.'

Doug isn't Mr. Tilney or Mr. Bingley; in trying to save Gina he must be a young and handsome version of Colonel Brandon.

'Rowland almost ruined me. But that's another story. His mother and mine were good friends for decades – my Mom helped the family a lot, but that is all forgotten now. Never mind. I don't bear grudges. It's Gina I care about.' Doug said, going back to his laptop, zooming in and out of our likenesses upon the screen. 'There – that's you, Jane Austen. I think you look great. If you get an opportunity, will you speak to Gina? I was reading up about you when we were putting this list together and you're a confirmed expert on affairs of the heart. I would so appreciate it.'

Cass, I promised him that I would try, though I do not know the Terminology of Today's Lovers, I suppose I shall get by somehow. Doug and Gina were an *Item,* and Rowland Hatton is a *Jerk.*

Yours ever

Jane

Later still!

I will just take a few minutes while we wait – this time '*House Beautiful*' does the office of a desk, and I hope I shall not have to give it up. The paintings are very interesting. The homes depicted on the pages inside are all light and colour and sleekness. This is how the Gentry live in 2016.

After my conversation with Doug, I was hurried back to the Hall, where we were gathered into our groups for our Destinations. We are five; the Brontë Sisters from 1848 (their Father is Irish, and there is a third sister and a brother at home) a Mr. Thackeray from 1855 who, having visited Limerick once, wishes to see it again; Miss Edgeworth who I hope will come to appreciate my work as many *discerning readers of no mean understanding* have already done, and myself.

In the Wardrobe Room we found cloathes we could decently wear, finding we need not show all our legs, but we rather miss our hats, because now we must dress our hair. Happy the hair one can hide under a hat! Whatever little resentment I have felt toward Miss Edgeworth has been put away for now; for we were both in need of a sister as we examined the odd garments, so different from what we are used to, and no stays to be had. We both of us laughed heartily at everything. The gentlemen in the next room cannot fail to have heard us.

Suitably dressed in 'separates' – gowns with bodice separately worn from the skirts – happy thought indeed! – we paraded ourselves back to the Hall. We have not a pocket-book between us, and wonder what we are to do for pewter. The pink bag we were given contain various items of interest, namely soft tissue passing as handkerchiefs – soap, a brush for teeth, and a tube of 'toothpaste' and a wax stick which is called 'deodorant', (it is this which Rena says we *must* use) and some items particularly for use by ladies. A wire-bound notebook, a 2016 calendar featuring kittens, a bottle of pills for pain relief. (why those? Miss Edgeworth is rummaging for a bottle of sal-volatile. I would favour lavender water. But no salts?)

As we waited to see what we were to do next, we got acquainted with each other a little more.

I learned that the Miss Charlotte Brontë has written a novel (and she is not ashamed to call it so) named *Jane Eyre*, which came out last year to excellent reviews. Miss Emily has written a novel also, *Wuthering Heights*, which sold very well. Mr. Thackeray – a bespectacled man in his forties - has quite an enviable list – *Vanity Fair*, which is set around the time of the Battle of Waterloo – that is the first one he is really happy with, for he has been a hack journalist, and *Vanity Fair* has freed him to write as he pleases. I am happy at least that the novel has Arrived, and I am rather proud to think of myself as having helped to make it Respectable. Mr. Thackeray is certainly more talkative than either of the Brontës, and we have had a good conversation. Miss Edgeworth listened carefully; perhaps she now will discard her reservations about novels, though from something else she has said, it appears that this opinion is not all her own, but that of her Father, who seems to think that novels are frivolous. She lives with him, and her brothers and sisters are very numerous, and though many are married and moved away, she had a hand in the education of almost all.

We are a little more friendly, since she spoke of how he always encouraged her, and I spoke of how our Father was so proud of all I have written – though I concluded that Mr. Edgeworth has too much influence over *her* writing, and bids her to alter it when he thinks fit. When I hear her speak of such fondness of him, I wish again that we still had our Beloved Father. He left us too quickly…How fleeting life is.

Your affectionate sister, Jane

My dear Cassandra

I am pleased to tell you that we have arrived in Ireland, but not at all pleased to tell you that I have little memory of the journey, we have had no travel adventures, no overturnings of the carriage, no Inn with damp sheets; nothing except a walk down another narrow corridor which led to a strange, round roofless circular chamber, and overhead a sky full of stars. We were bidden to sit in armchairs very deep and soft, the lights were extinguished and again I found myself in that place between wakefulness and sleep. That cannot be as interesting to you as a dinner of spoiled mutton and an indifferent Innkeeper who took all my money.

I awoke this morning to a piercing whistle, followed by a *chug-chug*, which went on for a few minutes until it faded away. It was dark, and I thought that there must be a table by my bed, with taper and candle, but though my hand easily found the small table, there was no candle. Another whistle followed in a few minutes, and then another. It began to lighten, and I was too affrighted to stir. Where was I? Then I began to hear a succession of harsh, roaring sounds, each beginning soft as a whimper, then growing in intensity until it seemed to explode in my ear, then fading again to a whimper, to be followed by another, and another – until there were many all together, and I was still too affrighted to get up and go to the window. I noted that I was still in my travelling cloathes. I opened my eyes wide when the light was coming straight in through a crack in the curtains, and saw that I was in a small oblong room, tastefully decorated in blues and whites.

I got up and went to the window, pulling the curtain a little aside to peep out. I was on the second floor and looking upon a street.

My eyes met an unbelievable sight. In place of horses, carts and carriages I saw only the carriages, and they were all colours, all closed, and appeared to go by themelves at incredible speeds. These were the sources of the roars.

There was not a horse in sight. But I saw a Park across the street, and at least the sight of trees and bushes, now in their Autumn colours, held some familiarity.

I do not want to use up all of the paper I have found in the room; suffice it to say that the fireplace is bricked up; but has a pretty screen in front of it - it is only September however and no fire is needed. A carpet goes wall-to-wall. I have all of the furniture I wish for, except a bookcase, and there is something in the ceiling with a glass globe in it - a kind of modern chandelier? Perched precariously upon a high shelf is a shiny big black box with little buttons on the side. I do not know it's purpose and I would cover it with my shawl if I had one. All will be explained, but now I have to find a 'bathroom', as explained in our Book of Instructions, which I perused while waiting for my Likeness to be taken.

There are two doors in this room. The first one I open leads into a bathroom. I have this all to myself? There must be some error, and perhaps Miss Edgeworth must come along to use it as well, and the Brontë sisters. The arrangements are beyond belief; an ingenious flushing system, hot water running from a tap!

An hour later: There! I have bathed! I got the fright of my life; in the bath, there is a long pipe with a drooping head like a sunflower, and I turned a knob, and a spray of cold water came from the head and down upon my unsuspecting head! I have wet my hair through.

We only have one set of cloathes - and wonder if we are to be given some stuff to make some – I must leave off – I hear the voices of my fellow companions upon the landing, so I must beg to finish – Yours affect - JA.

Later – still Tuesday

Dear Cassandra,

Behold me going to write you as long a letter as I can, to use up all the paper I have and then pine for more. *House Beautiful* did not journey with me; they must have pried it from my hand while I slept. I hope to make you very jealous of my account of today, though you will never see it. I shall start to bore you with Food.

An incomparable breakfast awaited us in a bright dining room facing the back garden. We ate bacon rashers, sausages, eggs, a delicious blood pudding, buttered toast and delectable brown soda bread. Everybody except Miss Emily did the table justice. Emily did not eat anything in New York yesterday and Miss Edgeworth has taken it upon herself to urge her to taste something, but Miss Brontë has said: 'We are indebeted to you, Miss Edgeworth, but my sister does not eat well when away from home'. Home is Yorkshire. Miss Emily hardly spoke, and when she did it was to mention Keeper, her dog, in a low voice to her sister. Miss Brontë informed me that when approached by Gina she consented readily to Time Travel, and since the sisters had travelled together before (to Brussels!) she made the request of Gina that Emily be asked along as well. So you see, Cass, I am a very bad sister, for I never thought to ask if you could come with me. Think of that today and grieve for your error in choosing me for your relative.

Our house is in Pery Square. There is a very pretty clock tower, a bank and a church. The Park is very elegant, with a fine entrance, good walks, and hills that children may roll down, as we used to do at Steventon. There is a pretty folly which is used as a bandstand, a water fountain, and a tall monument. I know all this because we visitors left the house before breakfast for a walk there, and passed the carriages close-up – smoke comes out the back of them via a little pipe. We are near to a school, for we met some schoolchildren in long maroon uniforms and packs upon their backs.

The house was built in the time of King George 1V; our present Regent - but it is not unlike, from the outside, our house in Bath. There is a front parlour, and the dining room may open from that, allowing the two rooms to become one – a recent alteration, designed for large companies of visitors. (It would be good for a Ball). The kitchen is below stairs; the coal cellar underneath the street. A path from the back of the house leads to the Carriage House and Stables. There must be Horses there!

Mary is our Hostess; she is a nice, comfortable kind of woman who keeps guests in summertime, but who has never had Time Travellers before. We are supposed to call her Mary, though that does not go well with us, as we would think she deserving of the title Mrs. Devane. She is all attention, though someone has impressed upon her that we are not to nose about in books concerning History or Biography, and she has hid all she has in the house except for a few modern novels. Her husband Eric, a jovial man, runs an 'Antique' Shop, and likes to collect old things, so I think we must be very welcome, and must take care he does not carry us off to display in his window.

The house Hums. Yes, it hums. I shall find out the explanation for this at the earliest opportunity. Everybody hears it, and we all find it disturbing, but nobody wishes to mention it, for fear of giving offence. The hum begins abruptly and ends in the same way, and then begins again. There are also mysterious clicks from time to time; whirrs and gurgles too. Every time somebody has used the water closet, you can hear the disturbance all over the house, and we do not remark it to each other. All of our rooms have an object beside the bed that, if you disturb it, lights up and hums also. There are a set of numbers on it. I suppose I will learn it's purpose, in the meantime it is in my way. We were subjected to another ferocious Noise just after breakfast and saw a servant come into the dining-room pushing a long, narrow machine in front of her. There was a tube of glass in its middle, and dust and dirt appeared to be whirling about in there. It sucked up our crumbs from the carpet. It was Deafening.

Gina appeared about ten o'clock (wearing today a wide-necked torquise wool chemise and the black hose again, with ankle boots.) She smiled brightly, looked about at us all, and hoped we slept well - and we hoped the same for her - she said she 'didn't sleep very well.' I suppose she has been awake juggling her thoughts between Doug and Rowland. I must find an opportunity to broach the subject with her, but feel I am not sufficiently acquainted. She gave us pocketbooks containing five hundred Euros, this being the currency here. We are quite delighted with our fortunes. So easily made, all we had to do was fall asleep. I quite fail to convert this currency into Pounds or Guineas. Here it is all the Metric system, as in France.

And that is not the only similarity with France, I hate to say, and it was disconcerting to find out – that Ireland has gone the way of America, and become a Republic. It is ours no more. In fact, Brittania has shrunk greatly since our Time. India is gone back to India, the West Indies rules itself. The places we sent our convicts to are now part of what is called the British Commonwealth, and they are prosperous in their own right. New South Wales and the other Penal Colonies now flourish with the descendants of those transported for crime. If matters had gone against our Aunt Leigh Perrot and the card of lace, she might have been transported for several years. What a pitiful goodbye it would have been for all of us, her family! Now it seems young people go there in droves to make their fortunes, and live high indeed, enjoying the sea-bathing and tennis. Such a turnabout! Who could predict it?

But I am very sad to report that our proud Navy is greatly diminished – do not mention it to Frank or Charles. Oh, here I am, writing as if you are going to receive this letter, which will never be – but as I bide here, I forget I shall be home before morning. But back to my subject - Mr. Thackeray is very surprised to hear that our power in the world is not what it used to be; for in his day, 1855, England's position in the world seems very secure indeed. America holds the distinction of that position now. America, of all places! It appears that the poor people of Europe have gone there in their millions, and their descendants have become very rich and made it the most powerful nation on earth.

We assumed that Gina had missed breakfast, but she went down to the kitchen and reappeared carrying a plate of toast and a cup of coffee. Mary came up to us – we were assembled in the front parlour – designated especially for guests, it has several easy chairs, a fireplace and the ugly shiny black box above it, similar to what is in our rooms but a great deal larger. The rest of the room is quite tasteful, with thick cream curtains and luxurious Turkish rugs, and a few interesting prints upon the walls. To get back to what I was about to write - Mary told us that if we were hungry at any time, we were to get ourselves a cup of tea or coffee – she brought us down to the kitchen, all gleaming and neat and no fire at all – and showed us how to put on the kettle and where the tea and coffee was kept. It is not locked up – she was amazed at the thought of its being locked up when Miss Edgeworth asked how we were to obtain the key. She goes home at seven after we have dined; our evening tea we are to make for ourselves. If we wake in the night and 'feel like a cup of tea' we may come down and make one for ourselves. She did however emphasise not to touch anything electric with wet hands, and that everything we 'plug in' must be 'unplugged' after use. I should be terrified to use anything electric, but I am sure I shall get over this after being 'electrocuted' the first time, which is apparently what happens people who are careless in 2016. I do not quite comprehend the meaning of the word but I am quite afraid of it, as it has five syllables.

The first scheme of ours is that we are to go to a shop and choose cloathes. Cloathes ready-made! What a delight! Have you not often heard me wish for some? The items we were given are ill-fitting; though my 'skirt' has no buttons, but an ingenious metal clasp that you pull with a tiny handle to close it. I must leave off for now – we are to meet downstairs for our first Adventure.

Later:

We walked out – the 'traffick' loud in our ears, looking with amazement at the people travelling at such speeds in the equipages, and an occasional long giant of a car, hung very high, holding many people in rows all facing forward. I asked Gina what the 'whistle and chug-chug' heard this morning could have been, for these 'cars' did not make that kind of noise, and Mr. Thackeray and Miss Brontë, together, were very quick in naming it 'a train', a vehicle that travels upon an iron roadway, very fast indeed, from city to city, carrying people in numerous coaches all linked together. 'How many Horses?' 'None,' they said with triumph, 'there is a Steam Engine pulling the Coaches', whereupon Gina corrected them and said Steam was gone now. But they have all traveled on a train, and Miss Edgeworth and I will have to wait several years more before we see them. They have quite the upper hand of us.

Our destination was a 'Department Store', named 'Wearables'. I walked beside Mr. Thackeray, (he is and will be Mr., for I cannot call him William) He is very happy to be back in Limerick, and notes all of the streets in Newtown Pery where we are lodged. They are pretty houses to be sure, and look new to me, though are old to Limerick. He confided to me *sotto voce* that he has met Miss Brontë in Real Life, and that he mistakenly introduced her to his mother by the name *Jane Eyre*, for which he was very much upbraided by her (the author) the following day. She was in London to meet *literati*, and when I asked if Emily accompanied her, he said no, then changed the subject.

He made particular enquiries of Eric – Mr. Devane – this morning about how things work and learned that Electricity is responsible for Everything of modern power and convenience. And to think we thought it only as a cure to be had at a watering-place, and a very dubious cure at that! So more than that I will not explain to you – how the cars run, how the streets and rooms are lit, how the dinner cooks, how the food is kept cold or warm. If I think that my words produce a puzzled look upon your brow, I shall add the letter 'E-tricity'. I am rather proud of my abbreviation; for I have heard many words begin with E nowadays. Gina talks of E-mail. Eric mentioned a Georgian Cruet he found on E-Bay. By the by, E-tricity accounts for the interminable Hum).

But dear Cassandra, you know why Limerick is of particular interest to *me*. I have not mentioned his name for a long time, but now I shall. Tom Lefroy. Do you remember a letter I wrote to you the day after the Ball at Manydown? (it was your 23rd Birthday, and you were away at the Fowles) I delighted in telling you of the happiness of the Ball; the words I believe I wrote to you about the

41

behavior of Tom and myself - *'imagine everything profligate and shocking and sitting down together'*. I was in a transport of joy, for I believed myself to be in love – and I believed he felt the same – but our attachment was of course noted, and talked of with great concern, I am now certain, at Ashe Rectory, by his Uncle and Aunt. Then how swiftly he was borne away from me, whisked away from poor penniless Jane to safety! Do you remember when a few years later he was visiting Ashe again, and great care was taken we should *not* meet? Had it not been for Father's discreet enquiry, I would have not learned that he had left for Ireland, for good. Any hope I had left of him returning to claim me, died then and there. I shall not dwell upon that.

But memories of our happy times flood my mind this morning, for I am in the city where *he* was born. I want to see his House if it still stands, the Church he worshipped in, the Assembly Rooms he danced in. Is anything still there? And I feel I shall be justified in finding out what 'became' of him eventually. We know he is married to a rich woman from Wexford, his friend's sister. I do not think it will be of any harm to find out if he 'did' well in his profession, and I mean to follow it, and find out how far he got in it, for I do not have the patience to wait decades in Chawton for news to trickle in about the doings of the Irish Lefroys, for that may never come. He may have done very well; he may not. I have always wished him well, in any case. How I wish you could answer me, to advise me. Your judgment is always sound, though I might not always take it. I have an opportunity – for if he made a name for himself, *Limerick* would know of it. But I am already excited to be in Limerick, as if something in the air will bring him to me again, for good or ill. His home is also in Newtown Pery, in Georges St, Number 108 – it must be only a short distance away.

But to our shopping, and an odd little incident - Wearables Stores is a vast warehouse filled with all kinds of goods upon display on racks for shoppers to rummage about and choose items for themselves. Nobody waits upon you, bringing you this and that, showing you the merchandise, so under Gina's guidance we females proceeded to the Ladies Wear, to hundreds of garments upon racks, but we were very disappointed in what we found, for everything is very ill-made. Poor material, loose threads, raw edges etc. I pointed this out to Gina, but she seemed surprised, and said it is the usual way in shops of this sort. What needlework! I should be ashamed to own it! I felt a little vexed, and Miss Brontë, Miss Emily and Miss Edgeworth wished to leave without delay, for the music from upstairs was irritating to them. It appears that the business has an orchestra playing somewhere, songs and concertos in styles entirely new and lacking melody. Raspy voices, forced, throaty, screechy...all peculiar and unpleasant to our ears. I was examining a new outer bodice (simply called a Top) and Miss Edgeworth fancied a sort of round gown, a billowing kind of 'dress' which would look dreadful on her dumpy figure, only I did not like to tell her so - when an odd thing happened; a woman's voice was singing, I was not listening to the words, but Miss Emily suddenly turned abruptly as if shot, dropped the cloathes she had in her hand, and gasped – 'She speaks of Heathcliff! That song is about my Heathcliff! And my Cathy! Charlotte! Listen!'

Gina was a little way off, staring at a small metal object that I have noticed she carries constantly and talks and taps onto – a tiny laptop...many people carry them so they do not even look where they are going – so she did not immediately hear - but a few people looked at Emily in surprise (do you know I almost wrote Marianne? She reminds me of my Marianne Dashwood! All sensibility!)

Miss Brontë cast her head toward the upstairs, her eyes bright with excitement – 'Yes, yes! It is indeed a song about *Wuthering Heights!*'[2]

'But how can they treat it so?' Shouting, screeching noises! I must go to the musicians!' Emily said with determination, stepping upon the dress now on the floor. 'Where is the staircase?'

Gina had by now noticed what was happening, and hurriedly replacing her tiny laptop in her bag, she rushed to Emily.

'Oh Emily! Please be careful with the merchandise!' she said.

'Take me to that singer upstairs,' Emily said with great agitation. 'I wish to speak with her! She has no right to sing about *my* moors, *my* inventions!'

'There is no singer upstairs,' Gina had to almost shout to make Emily pay heed, and I was surprised also to find that out, for the music most assuredly came from an upstairs floor. 'That's a Recording!'

'What is the explanation for the singing?' I demanded to know.

Gina told us that it was possible in these times to Capture Audio. Someone speaking, someone singing, a dog barking – it can all be 'captured' on a device – she pulled out her tiny laptop.

'See my I-Phone? Listen!' She tapped something quickly. 'Say something,' she commanded me, holding it toward me. 'Go on, Jane!'

'*The family of Dashwood had been long settled in Sussex,*' I said, after a brief pause. Gina tapped another few times, and then we heard

---

[2] Emily is hearing Kate Bush's hit song from 1978 named 'Wuthering Heights.'

my voice, with the exact words I had spoken reproduced to perfection. We were stunned.

After we had purchased skirts, dresses, tops, jackets and *lingerie* enough, (I will tell you about *that* when I get home, if I remember, but there was a great deal of *giggling*) we were taken to buy shoes, where we were bidden to sit and be waited upon while we were fitted. Some of the shoes look like glorified pattens, and the square toes of many others are not at all elegant! But we made our choices. We need hats and gloves, for we do not feel dressed going out without them, but we had to return to the house.

Miss Edgeworth and I discussed the Audio Capture as we walked back. 'We have echoes in Nature,' she said, 'if you say 'halloo!' in a quarry, the halloo comes back to you – it is the same principle, I warrant.'

'Perfected by Electricity', I said, and we left it at that. Another modern mystery.

Miss Edgeworth thinks Gina makes a dreadful appearance, with a complexion of bronze, a carmine mouth and dramatic colours about her eyes like Cleopatra, and of course her nails painted. She would set her down as a Dasher[3], but I will not allow it. I defend Gina; she is no different than all of the other young ladies we have seen, they all wear paint. I am prepared to overlook what appears to be excess, because she is very prepared to like us, odd as *we* must be. She speaks with a frankness that is appealing, has an open and affectionate nature, and reminds me of our nieces. And though I am completely in ignorance about modern fashion, I would say that there is a certain harmony about her look. But even I do not understand why she sports a little tattoo. It says

---

[3] A fast young woman.

'*segui il tuo cuore*' and has a little red flower trailing after it. 'Follow your heart' - which is an excellent message to write upon your skin if you must write something. I must finish - Yours affctly…Jane

Dear Cassandra

The City of Limerick has an abundance of charm, and the people very friendly. After lunch, with the sun shining on this golden autumn day, we went out again and down to the Shannon River, saw three fine bridges and pretty strands on the opposite bank. Miss Edgeworth sighed over the Shannon, and said that if there were a boat about she would like to sail upriver to her house in County Longford. She asked Eric (who accompanied us) if he knew if the Edgeworths still lived there. He said he thought not. She seemed very disappointed to hear that, and I suppose she thought they had fallen upon hard times and had to sell. But it appears that many great houses are not inhabited anymore by old families. She enquired of her neighbours at Pakenham Hall, also in Longford. She said that she knows Miss Catherine Pakenham that was, who married the Duke of Wellington. The Brontës jumped to hear of the connection; the Duke is their idol. Eric said he was familiar with the Pakenham name and was sure the family was still there, living in a portion of the house, for no family can afford to run a Castle nowadays, except a Rock Star. It appears, Cass, that the Rock Stars are *musicians and singers, composers and performers* of the music we have heard today, and one such owns and lives in a Castle in Dublin, and a famous Dancer lives in another in County Cork.

(My Poor Pemberley! Is it similarly afflicted? Do the descendants

46

of the proud Darcys huddle in a few small rooms of their Great House? Indeed Mr. Darcy would be very gravely troubled, after the care and attention he has lavished upon his house and fine gardens! Or does a Rock Star live there?) But what of famous Chatsworth now? Is that Mansion merely a museum thrown open to the publick? And Godmersham? Surely our brother has descendants enough to keep it open.

Mr. Thackeray is similarly stricken with the changes wrought by Time, though in a different, and very good way. The last time he was in Limerick, he was besieged by urchins. He had marked the starved, ragged townspeople, and written of them in '*The Irish Sketches.*' He could not be more astonished. But he had one grave disappointment; his former Inn, Cruises, which was, he described, one of the best he had ever seen, is now completely gone. 'Not a stone left of its fine entrance!' he cried. There are shops in its place. He is quite disgusted, for he knew Mr. Cruise, who took great pride in his Hotel. It had been a bustling place, a meeting place for the City and County gentry, and the point from where the Stagecoach left every morning for Dublin. There is however, a bookshop, Easons, near where it stood, so that was a little consolation.

Later, when we were home again, Eric got his laptop and brought it over to the table where Miss Edgeworth sat. I heard her exclaim: 'My word, that *is* Pakenham Hall!' I joined them, and we sat and watched Eric put the laptop through its paces, a click here, a tap there, brought us different views of the Castle and fine lawns on the inside of the lid, and of people enjoying themselves on the lawns and in the woods.

'So many children about!' said Maria. 'They are not tenants' children, surely, allowed to run about and play everywhere? I am sure the Head Gardener would have a strong objection.'

Eric was tapping and bringing up different blocks of information and pictures, and we could hardly keep up with him.

'It appears that the Head Gardener, as you call him, is Lord Longford himself,' he said. 'You have to understand how Big Houses work nowadays. They have to be open to the public to survive. So you see – there are all these public events at the Castle, races, shows, concerts, all to bring in money. And look – he clicked again – 'there's a tearoom in the stables.'

'A tearoom in the stables!' we exclaimed in disbelief.

Miss Edgeworth was astonished beyond belief, as I was. 'Eric, I must ask you to conduct me to Longford so that I can see Pakenham Hall, and my own house at Edgeworthstown, for myself! Perhaps I may call upon Lord and Lady Longford.'

She spoke with a peremptory air – she means no harm by it; it is her way, and usual for somebody of her Rank – but I felt Eric bristle momentarily, and he answered politely: 'I have business in the next few days – Mary will drive you to Longford, I'm sure!'

'Mary!' we chorused in amazement. Women do not drive women long distances. Not in our Time.

'Mary!' he called out, and she came up from the kitchen. 'Maria here wants to go to Longford. Will you take her up?'

'Longford, is it? Well it depends on the day, but I suppose I can,' was the reply. 'I'll have to get my mother over to keep an eye on the children after school.'

'If people drink tea in the stables, I am sure they stable the horses elsewhere,' Miss Brontë said.

Eric laughed. 'If they still have them. This would be a converted

48

stables. In fact – you have probably seen the carriage-house and stables at the end of the garden here. That's where my wife and I live, and our children, a boy and a girl. It's all converted, of course. It's all modern inside. Every mod con you can think of.'

'But why did you not pull it down and build a proper House?' asked an astonished Mr. Thackeray.

'Oh we didn't want a modern house. We liked the look of the building,' said Mary who had sat down in the parlour with us. Now she invited us – urged us - to visit. And so we got up and followed her out the front door, and around to the alley to the main entrance. (they use the garden path to go back and forth during the day) We came to what is a Carriage House to all appearances upon the outside, but what a surprise awaited us when we went in the door large enough to admit a good-sized coach. A very charming hall and stairs of gleaming wood and soft amber lighting, with brightly coloured draperies and furnishings, and a great deal of pottery. She was immensely proud of it, and showed us the kitchen, parlours and bedrooms – we met her daughter Lisa in her maroon uniform who was sitting like a Buddha upon her bed, with her laptop. She smiled but did not get up to greet us, and Mary said she was doing her homework – she was in 'Junior Cert'. Miss Edgeworth drew near and asked her what subject she was engaged in – 'Home Economics' which pleased her. The boy's bedroom was untidy, adorned with giant pictures of athletes and red banners proclaiming 'Manchester United'. Passing though the kitchen again, we saw the boy helping himself to food.

'Charlie, rinse the plate when you are finished, won't you? And put it in the dishwasher. Charlie, these guests are Time Travellers.'

49

'Yes, Mam. And I'm a Ninja.'

'Now there we are' Eric said as we made our way back to the tall red-brick house via the back garden. 'Did you ever see a stables like that in your life?'

'They value now what we held in no account at all,' Miss Edgeworth whispered to me.

'It is the modern version of the Picturesque,' I whispered back. 'Burned-out abbeys from the Reformation enchant us; Stables enchant them.'

'But I am very curious as to how a girl would learn 'Home Economics' from a machine,' she added. 'and not to get up and greet us, and to learn sitting upon the bed, of all places! How very odd there is not a room – or a table at least - dedicated to the children's education! It is all so *laissez faire* nowadays!'

Before I leave off about Stables, Cass, I have to add the following - there is not a Horse to be seen anywhere. How peculiar the street, how odd the city, the road, without the familiar clip-clop! I miss their neighs and snorts, I miss the smell of horsehair, the big beloved dumb faces, the tossing manes. Any horse odour would be preferable to us than the fumes we inhale from the cars. Have I ever lived one day of my life before without seeing a horse?

Your affectionate sister, Jane

Wednesday September 21st

Dear Cassandra

How I spoil you with letters you will never get. I hope you appreciate it and reward me tomorrow by mending my green sash. Speaking of which, we begged scissors, needles and thread from Mary and have whipped our seams into better shape. I will tell you more of the cloathes we purchased – morning wear in the shape of long skirts, tops and jackets; and dresses – long of course – for evening. Shawls are not to be got, but there are 'wraps' or what are termed 'cardigans' to go over the gowns. Jackets for the outdoors – again one for everyday, and a good one for Sunday. Tippets - termed *Scarves* - for about our necks, and stockings – these last only reach the knee but hold themselves up! None of us has the courage to wear Trousers or Breeches as modern women do.

We have been in 2016 now for two days, and it is time I wrote more about food. Breakfast is very good, as I have said, but dinner disappointing. The meat has a blandness, the garden stuff without much taste. Great care is taken to disguise that meat comes from a creature with a Head, and so far we are denied the pleasure of any Cranium stuffed with delectables. Legs and Wings abound, but we have yet to see a Liver, a Kidney or a Tongue! Mrs. D – Mary – serves a tasty sauce, but it does not agree with me, being too rich, though I have not been ill since I came here. All of the garden stuff is got from the shops. However, ice cream is available all year round, and that is delightful!

Mary has but one servant to help her, and that is only because we are so many, she says that normally she does not keep any, and none in her house. Anna is from Poland, is not called a servant, but 'a Girl Who Comes In To Help' and speaks only a little English. She dresses our beds and tidies our rooms; helps to prepare food and clean up after, but she is not at our beck and call.

We five guests have delightful conversations, as we all share a love for literature. We discuss the Poets and Writers of our Times, and our mealtimes pass very quickly. Miss Emily, though I understand her to be a poet of extraordinary talent, does not profess any interest in other writers. She listens quietly, but her grey eyes rarely meet ours, and she often looks away when she must speak. However she is in better spirits. She has made friends with a big black shaggy dog in the Park, and goes there to run with it. I have not discussed my work with Miss Edgeworth again; I feel it is a subject better left alone. We long to visit a bookshop! But it is strongly discouraged, though not forbidden.

Rena paid us a visit, and when we asked her about the above, she mentioned a famous General who Time-Travelled the night before a battle, and he went to the History Section and found out that he had been defeated. He was very reluctant to return to his tent. With regard to looking for our own works in the bookshops, Rena cautioned us – she said that almost the first things we would see would be a biographical note on the author. Who wants to come by the date we were taken from this world? It may be that thread that remains after we return. We all saw the wisdom of what she was saying, but I doubt we can pass the bookshops anymore than a dog can pass a bone.

The Devanes bookshelves are of limited interest; the modern novels are very fast and racy, the love scenes go very far beyond what is decent. *Tom Jones* is not even in the running. We doubt we would have any success nowadays with ours, if there is a required love scene with graphic descriptions of how it is all accomplished. Miss Edgeworth and I asked Mary for a volume of poetry. She said that poetry is hardly read now, but she would obtain a book for us – whereupon her daughter lent us her Schoolbook, full of delightful verse, much of it familiar, and some very pleasing new works, some by Americans – Robert Frost, for instance, and an Irish poet named William Butler Yeats – 'admirable!' in Miss Edgeworth's judgement. But no Cowper! Is he out of fashion? For

Shame! But I have made an Extract from Frost, and Miss E from Yeats.

We are to be relieved of all we collect before we return; as it would confuse the Antiquarians, and they must not be able to dig a self-inking pen out of the ruins of Chawton Cottage in the year 3000. So I may not hide any in my pockets to take back. Our writings, also, must be taken from us and 'shredded' in a machine.

Every neighbourhood must have a Family of consequence, and if there is one here, Miss Edgeworth will find it out. But all of her enquiries about Families of significance have met with bewilderment in our hosts. They have offered the Mayor as the First Citizen, but that is not exactly what Miss Edgeworth means. She wants Landed Gentry. The species appears to be almost extinct.

But to tell you our scheme today - we walked a short distance through the city to King John's Castle. It is a very fine edifice, sitting upon a bank of the Shannon River, and the bustling city comes and goes about its feet. It is now owned by the Irish Government. We received a full History, which the man in medieval costume who calls himself a 'Re-Enactor', was happy to give, including battles and long bloody sieges. The Brontës were in raptures, for there is nothing they like better than a good Battle. They peered through every chink in the walls and clambered under the barriers and into the excavations, the better to relive the experience. The interior is an exhibition area – 'admirably done! - ' Miss Edgeworth says. It is a favourite phrase with her, if she finds something to her liking. We all of us climbed to the Battlements, and we had a treat there – a magnificent view of the River winding its way about the City like a silver serpentine path. We walked back by an area in which Gina, armed with a book about Limerick, pointed out various interesting ruins, including a wall of ivy-clad Tuscan coloumns which is all that is left of the old Custom House. We walked a little farther to the bank of the Abbey River, and came by the site of the old Assembly Rooms. There is nothing left of the original building. Still, I stood and stared, and tried to imagine the moonlit nights when the water gleamed, and the carriages drew up, and the families alighted, many having driven in from the country as we did when we went to Basingstoke - the young people all excitement, anticipation and chatter – the older full of cautionary words, and all the 'yes, Mamas,' said without any attention, upon hearing the orchestra, and espying the head of a friend, or her handsome brother. Then all proceeding to the Ballroom, which would have been provided with the usual tea, card and supper rooms, as well as a very good well-lit room for dancing. Gina's book says that the ballroom was very roomy, had a coved ceiling, and cut-glass wall brackets for candles. It would have been a great sight, and I am perfectly sure I would have danced a happy quadrille here on Assembly Mall, as the new Bride of Mr. Thomas Lefroy!

But while my mind is upon the events of over 200 years ago, others in the party wish to view the more modern buildings, and we walk to a modern Tower which appears to be made of glinting glass, and beyond that, imagine a round white tower with rows of wide windows (oh, if there is window tax, the owner must be distressed indeed!). The tower appears to be missing part of it's top wall, making the side by the river shorter than the other. This is the Clarion Hotel. Inside, Gina persuades us to take 'the elevator' or 'the lift' as I heard somebody else call it, and my heart in my mouth, I step inside and am closeted up with several other people as we shoot up through the building, and down again. I am very relieved to be spilled into the lobby once again, for tales of walled-up rooms are uppermost in my mind, thanks to the horrid novels of Mrs. Radcliffe.

Mr. Thackeray's mind is on his dinner, so we turn for Pery Square, and dined upon boiled bacon and cabbage, floury potatoes and parsley sauce. Our evenings will be spent in the parlour, if there is no play or concert. Last even Miss Edgeworth and I made the tea for the rest of our party; it was quite an adventure filling the kettle from the tap and putting it on to boil. We made sure we 'unplugged' everything before we took the tea things up.

Then it is upon us to amuse ourselves for the even until bedtime. We have at our disposal a pack of cards, a piano, a game of letters named 'Scrabble' and the Television above the mantelpiece. This is another, more advanced use of Capture than the Audio I wrote of earlier. Today it is possible to act a play, capture the sound and movement for display later, and 'run' this play upon Television. This is the ugly shiny black thing hanging in the front parlour, in my room and indeed in everybody's room. When you press a button, it bursts into life in colour and sound.

I have begun to call it the Little Theatre. It is very noisy and it's flashing pictures hurt the eyes; the people talk very loudly and rapidly. There is little that we can see of grace or elegance in the Little Theatre. So we do not turn it on except for a programme called 'Nationwide' which Miss Edgeworth likes, for it features the Towns of Ireland, and also we view the Weather Forecast, and are rapt at the person moving clouds and rainfall about. Gina, (who goes out sometimes at night *on her own*, all dressed up, to meet a friend who works in '*the Airlines*' – wherever that is) does not sit with us, for it is her Time Off.

Gina neither plays nor sings, neither is she good with her needle. She laughingly replies that a girl does not have to have 'accomplishments' now, but an Education is essential, and we heartily agree, though all of us have horrible stories from Schools we attended. Poor Miss Edgeworth was stretched by her neck on a

55

regular basis in attempts to make her taller.

Last even, Mr. Thackeray took a walk, and I suppose visited the Tavern. We ladies played cards and Scrabble – a very clever game! Miss Emily did not join in. She took the tea tray down to the kitchen and washed the dishes and dried them. She spent a long time down there and I suspect she prefers her own company to that of any of us except for her sister Charlotte. Before we retire, we turn off the lights downstairs, and flick a switch that lights the staircase. How odd to climb to bed without a candle.

I have come to know my companions a little better. Miss Edgeworth spent her early years in Oxfordshire, returning to her Father's Estate in Longford at fourteen. She still visits England, is often in Society, and she has travelled in Europe. I am sure she writes gossipy letters to her Aunt, as I write to you! What does she write of Miss Jane Austen? The Brontës were teachers for a time, then set about beginning a school in their father's parsonage, but in their remote area of Northern England they did not receive any applicants, and so they decided to write books for publication. They sat around a table, all three girls after their father had gone to bed, and wrote every night, until all had completed their Novels – and they sold them. They pretended to be male.

I have got more writing paper. I never saw so much paper in my life. In the shop, I did not know what to choose, there was so much of it, and it is the fashion to place a letter in a little packet called an Envelope, rather than folding it as we do.

I am wishing tomorrow for an ox-cheek stuffed with dumplings, or a veal ragout, or cheese on toast; orange wine and tamarinds. I do not know how cheese on toast might be managed without a fire. There is a fireplace in the parlour but no grate; there is a sculpture of a pile of coal, and gas makes it glow. The flames leap about without a hiss or a crackle. Also, you cannot throw anything into it, and a Heroine would be hard put to destroy an incriminating note in a hurry, with a lover or a husband at the door. I am becoming used to using the Pen without stopping to dip it in ink, but at first I was pausing constantly, much to my own amusement. - Yrs affct, Jane

Thursday September 22nd

My Dear Cassandra

I have a few minutes to write before Lunch. It rained heavily this morning, and we ladies staid in hoping for a break in the weather. Idle from about ten o'clock, we asked Mary if she had any work for us to do, and she did not understand that we meant sewing and mending etc. so she suggested that if we wished to help, we could wash some Linen for her. We were completely taken aback. We summoned Gina, who reassured us that all we had to do was to bundle the Linen into a Machine, add Washing Powder and turn a knob to the type of Wash we desired. That we did, with much relief and enjoyment, under her direction. The Wash swirled about noisily and merrily for about forty minutes, and was rinsed without us doing anything further. After it was done, we took it out, and added it to a Dryer, and turned another knob. How Sally would love this! How easy the dreaded Mondays would be for her! Do not tell her or she will hate me and I will never get her to do anything for me again. [4]

We took to the task with gusto, and while we 'worked' we chatted

---

[4] Sally was the Austen servant at Chawton Cottage. Though she did not include servants as major characters in her novels, Jane's letters reveal that the servants were part of the family, and that their welfare was important to them.

with Gina. She begins to remind me a little of Cousin Eliza. She has the same vitality, loves her fashion, and has at times a theatrical air. She waves her hands about her a great deal when she talks.

All of this Activity took place in the basement, in a room beside the Kitchen, and we were a cozy group, as we made a pot of tea while the linens tumbled about in the Dryer. Next, it was time to Iron, and yes, E-tricity again – Miss Emily is very quick to discover the switches etc, and fiddled about with the iron to get it to a correct temperature, and Gina, dressed today in a narrow blackberry-coloured skirt to her knees with a riot of bright patterns – answered our questions about today's Fashions. I was bold and asked her about the hose that stops at the ankles; it appears they are called Leggings; the skirt she has on today is Pencil style. While the cloathes were drying she invited us to her room to see her wardrobe. Such a variety of little tops and little and long skirts, and long trousers! We were particularly admiring of a very long black soft silk-like dress overlaid with delicate lilac lace on the bosom – never mind that it had no sleeves at all - and a long loose white chiffon top that seemed to float. (We have to accept the terrible workmanship or we would like nothing). She also has *Sweddas* – that is knitted all-in-one tops with sleeves, that go on and off over the head. What a novel idea! So warm! Her jewellery is cheap but not gaudy; carefully chosen, and goes with nearly every outfit. She favours silver-(or perhaps plate) for earrings and bracelets, and some of her jewellery has almost a look of metal. She has little material of value; no silk for instance, and no fur at all, but the imitations today are very good. On her dressing-table was a glassy pink box overflowing with bottles of cosmetics and and sponges and the palettes of eye colours of which she is so fond. Foundation creams, mascaras, lipsticks, lip glosses, everything sparkly or matte, it seems - wads of cotton wool, brushes to apply! Little decorations for her nails! How much work it is to look pretty nowadays! (Miss Edgeworth's Lady Delacour would envy Gina her array). She explained every item, and we were greatly diverted, and she offered to make each of us up, and we succumbed to a little face foundation, and eyelid colour, and beheld ourselves in the mirror with shocked giggles. Oh and her hair does not need papers put in overnight – she has an Electric Curler for her spirals – a long stick that heats up and begets her curls.

'You must have a great deal to carry with you, and yet you move so quickly through Time and Space!' said Miss Brontë. 'How fast you must work!'

'Yes, and we have to go even faster now. They've cut back on our staff and we're stretched to the limit. When Rena was here the other day, she had a few words with me about my Performance. My new Quota is 100 clients per month, and make sure they are a good fit. You are all happy, aren't you?' she looked at us a little anxiously, and we reassured her that we were indeed happy.

'I have a co-worker who lies to get his numbers up. There was this poor kitchenmaid from 1860 or so, she was told she could get a really good job and bring her earnings back with her – of course she couldn't take anything back. She thought she'd never have to scrub again, poor thing, and wanted to start a flower-shop.'

We were very angry to hear that, and hoped the worker was punished, but were told that he was too 'in' with Top Management for anything to happen to him. And there was no way to prove it, in any case. He saw no harm in what he was doing; the maid would have no memory of any of it when she was to wake in the morning. And he exceeded his Quota and got an excellent Evaluation. 'He's a *Shvitzer*,' Gina said, her dark eyes

59

flashing, and we knew what she meant though we had never heard the word before. She was talking fast again, and went on:

'Rena told me that TTT brought in a team of Consultants called *Efficiency Plus* to work out how to save money. It costs a fortune to hire these people! One of their recommendations is to use only short, thin guests to save on printing costs, and another is to lose the Snickers at Orientation. Maybe I should go back to grooming dogs. I did that in college for extra cash.'

'You should get a better occupation,' Miss Brontë said, 'as far as I can tell, women can do anything they want now; for I saw a plaque with the name of a woman on it who was an attorney-at-law, and another who was a doctor!' The fact that most women earn money is astounding to us, and very pleasing. And it has struck us that there must be far more sickness today than before, because there are doctors and surgeons on every corner.

'And you should get married,' Miss Edgeworth urged, not understanding that if a woman has independence, she does not have to marry at all, like Emma Woodhouse. (I made that point in *Emma*, and she said she read the book!) 'Marry well; no dog grooming, no conduction of Time Travellers who do not know what they are about, and are afraid of the shower, like myself, and think they are going to smother every time they stand under the Sunflower.' (for this name I gave it has stuck).

We helped Gina hang her cloathes back in the wardrobe, and walked downstairs again.

'Just do not become a teacher or a governess,' Miss Brontë said darkly. I agree heartily, having seen our nieces and nephews torment poor Miss Sharpe.[5]

'Oh, come now, Miss Brontë,' said Mr. Thackeray, just coming in, for he had walked out, under the protection of the only umbrella in the house. 'Your experience brought you a wonderful autobiographical tale in – er - *Jane Eyre*. And your younger sister Miss Anne Brontë, with her book '*Agnes Grey*.' A story very well told, full of insight and, I am happy to say, a good ending. A wise and kind clergyman, Mr. Weston.'

Miss Edgeworth and I exchanged a glance. It is tiresome for people to talk of Books of the future which we could not possibly have read yet. Could we possibly find them?

'Is it continuing to sell in 1855 then?' Miss Brontë asked with eagerness, and Mr. Thackeray looked a little confused, as if he remembered now they have come from 1848, and he from 1855.

'And – *Wuthering Heights*?' Miss Emily asked, her colour heightened. 'I am writing another, but would like to know if I should continue, or just keep to my poetry.'

'Both - selling very well indeed,' he said, a little uncomfortably, and obviously not wishing to continue speaking of a future they did not know of, he addressed Gina, with whom he is, we think, a little charmed.

'Miss Gina, do people from this Century like to go back in Time?' he asked.

'A lot of modern people would like to go back. They want to fight in a famous battle or something. That we cannot do. Too

---

[5] Miss Sharpe was a governess who became a lifelong friend of Jane's.

dangerous. You'd be amazed at the things people want to do, but have no clue about what they might actually face. So we don't approach them. Some demand modern plumbing. Impossible.'

We all laughed. Somehow the idea of a modern person not having their usual amenities greatly amused us. Gina loudly protested: 'You guys are too cruel!' She is right of course.

So – now we are to have lunch, so I must finish – I have a scheme for myself for the afternoon, and intend to escape the company. You may wonder why I have not done it already -- Yrs, Jane

Still Thursday, 4pm

Dear Cassandra,

Later on: It still rained, but I walked out after Lunch, upon my mission. I could not find George's St! I asked several people, but nobody had heard of it! George's St., in Newton Pery! It could not be far!

Then I asked a gentleman of middle-age, a scholarly type, who I thought should know everything in the world, and he said: 'Goodness me, Mrs. - you are talking about O'Connell St! Where in the world did you get George's St? It hasn't' been called that for nearly a hundred years!'

I mumbled something about having seen a reference in a book, and he directed me to O'Connell St, and I realized I have walked down this street several times, O'Mahony's Bookshop is on it, and I may have passed number 108 several times.

But he was looking at me too curiously, and he said then: 'It was named after King George, and after Independence, it was named after Daniel O'Connell, the Liberator. You have heard of him?'

'Oh, no – I am afraid I have not.'

'A great man,' he said proudly. 'He won the Right for Catholics to sit in Parliament, and without striking a blow. But you are a visitor to Ireland, I see, so how would you know about that?'

Absolved, I went upon my way. It is true I do not know much about Irish affairs, except for the Rebellion of 1798 which Henry as you know had to go to Dublin for in his Militia days.

I soon reached 108 O'Connell St. I stood and stared at the building, dejected at the scene before me. The original house is gone; it is now a very modern square building full of glass and turquoise window frames, and it is a Bank. Allied Irish Bank.

I stood outside, quite disappointed, and yet not knowing why, or what I expected to find. A young descendant running out of a front door with *his* eyes, *his* hair?

This is a very busy corner of Limerick, and as I stood there, I realized that people were stepping around me to get to the Hole in the Wall that money comes out of. I was in the way of people wanting to get to it, so I began to walk away.

The children had been let out of school (all children go to school! It is the Law! Free Education!) they were congregating everywhere, the older boys and girls contriving to meet up in groups, and the younger ones with their mothers, having been let out a little earlier. All wear uniforms; brown, blue, green – very neat. Since I have come all this way, and the sky was clearing at last, I was determined to make something Lefroy-ish out of my walk, so I decided to find out if he had made something of himself, and if he was remembered in Limerick at all.

63

But how? A circulating library, perhaps, might be a useful place to visit. Again, I asked a passerby.

She looked a little puzzled and directed me then to 'the City Library.'

I set off briskly; waited at William St. Corner for *'the green man'* (a light that says you may cross) and off I went, down past Easons Bookshop, Cruises-that-was, and into Michael St. and round about it at the top, to see a fine brick building that used to be a Granary, and by the looks of it, is still proud of its origins. A Barnful of Books! Not knowing where to begin, I asked for help, and was soon looking up the index of a hefty volume about the Judiciary under British Rule.

Lefroy, Thomas Langlois – I found him. Firstly, a silhouette of an older man – every trace of youth gone. Lefroy, Thomas Langlois, Lord Chief Justice of Ireland.

Are you surprised, Cass? I was. But as I began to read his progress in his profession, the accolades, the words danced before my eyes, and I instantly felt an anxiety that I should not remember anything I read…so much I was not aware of…that the family is Heugenot I knew, and fled France in the sixteenth century, and they were silk dyers…merchants…his Father married the daughter of a penniless squire…why did that leap out at me? He took silk 1816, the year I am at in Real Life – nobody told the Austens yet! And now I go to the Future…

I asked for paper to make extracts from the pages, but the helpful clerk took the heavy book from me to copy the information out by means of a large machine, and the pages (yes, pages!) came out on a tray, reproduced to near-perfection. In fact, she thought it was rather too dark, and redid it, lighter. And I left the City Library clutching several pages to peruse in private, at home.

Cass – you know me as nobody else on earth does, and I wish I would remember all of this when I return, but I will not, and be as ignorant as ever.

But I knew I could spot a clever man, a Lord Chief Justice in the making. At least £10,000 pounds a year, don't you think? As rich as Mr. Darcy, I am sure of it! Did he have his own *Pemberley*? I shall find out. I shall leave off writing for a while, and take up my pen a little later on.

An Hour Later:

I feel overwhelmed, and not at all equal to taking in all the information I have acquired about Mr. Lefroy, but am quite intrigued to find out he has lived a long, useful life past Ninety. But first, the history, and an astonishing one, to me.

The Lefroys at Hampshire have a great secret about their family in Limerick, which I have found out today. It is this: *Tom's father Anthony Lefroy, an ensign in the 22nd Foot in Limerick, eloped with a penniless girl – a Miss Gardiner.* This marriage made his Uncle Benjamin Langlois (the same Uncle who paid for Tom's education) very angry with his nephew, but he forgave him and gave the marriage his blessing before Tom was born. At that time there were several daughters, and we know that several more children followed. Mr. Lefroy became a Captain during this time, and also purchased a command of the Dragoons in 1785. He was never wealthy, but his imprudent marriage did not cause him impecuniousness.

However this transgression of Mr. Anthony Lefroy must have caused consternation in the wider family – and I am sure served to make his brother at Ashe Rectory more sensible of the 'danger' his nephew was in when he visited Hampshire and distinguished penniless Miss Jane at Manydown and the other places where we were in company. It seems likely to me that Mr. Lefroy was forced to leave Hampshire and the danger of an imprudent match.

But here is my thought - I think the younger Mr. Lefroy may have done what his own father had done, and been forgiven as his father had been forgiven – and it may not have done him any harm at all.

After I had read this history, I felt very out of spirits, and wondered at the wisdom of my curiousity. I almost put the document out of my hand (I thought of the fire, but there is none of course) but like someone determined to be tortured, I read on.

That he returned to Ireland to practice Law we know, and that he married Mary Paul of Wexford we know also. He was very well thought of, coming to the notice of Lord Clare in 1802 (who is he? A man of great consequence, as John Dashwood would say). He served with distinction on the Munster Circuit, and Mr. Lefroy became *Kings Counsel*, in 1816. His eloquence impressed many distinguished people.

In time, Mr. Lefroy became very pious, and was seen to have 'a saintly look' at Bible Meetings. (This makes me wonder if he would have objected to novels as frivolous.)

I was surprised and a little amused to see that Mr. Lefroy settled on an Estate in County Longford, in a house named Carrigglass. He would become a neighbour to Miss Edgeworth; would that she had come from 1840 instead of 1816, and she could relate many a tale of the Lefroys. She could tell me if Mrs. Lefroy was intelligent and well-read, and how neatly she sewed her husband's shirts…but I must not allow my thoughts to run on in this ridiculous fashion.

He was elected to Parliament in 1830. How Mrs. Ferrars would have rejoiced had he been her son. Now he could drive a Barouche all over London - if he had gone there. He did not arrive in Parliament until 1831, and staid fifteen years.

The last piece of information I read of him is that he was *vehemently opposed* to Catholic Emancipation, and fought to keep Catholics from being Members of Parliament and from the Senior Judiciary, fearing, I suppose, that the power of the Protestant Church would be diminished.

All of this reading about Tom Lefroy returned me to those bittersweet times, and those feelings, of 1796. I greatly preferred him to any other man I had ever met, and I was certain he felt the same about me…I expected him to declare himself. Oh, there was no engagement. Like my Marianne Dashwood, I can say that there was no engagement. And no declaration of Love, but 'it was every day implied but no day professedly declared' – and when I wrote that I was to dance my last with Mr. Lefroy, I did not quite believe that myself. He would return. He would find me again. He would find a way. The feeling we had among us, that sharing of thought, of feeling, of being as one, which I knew he felt also – one cannot imagine this communication – a sensible person cannot be mistaken in this, and I never believed myself a Harriet Smith – Tom Lefroy was my soulmate! Yet, while I did not hear that he was married, I hoped.

And then came Bath, and I became certain at last that he was lost to me, for I am sure he was there, and we did not meet. And when we went to Town, and staid in Cork St, meeting old Mr. Langlois who did not distinguish me in the least, I knew the horrid truth – I had lost Tom. If old Mr. L had liked me, I think it would have gone well for Tom and me. But what was it about me that this old man did not like? Did he fear the intrusion of tall and slender

67

forms, or hazel eyes, or hair that curls itself, into the Lefroy line? Was I too forward, too intelligent, too reserved, or too stupid? I will never know, but I suspect that I was too *poor*.

'*Catharine or the Bower*' – how I cannot bear it now. I never look at it; it will never see print, not ever. I put it away, and then retrieved it from the shelve and in that flush of love for Tom in early 1796, rewrote it from my heart. If I remember any thread of this night, it will see the flames. You say it is good; I say I will never return to it. Edward is forced away from Catharine, and like Tom and Jane, the story ends at that point.

Why did Tom not fight for me, as his father had fought for his choice? I am quite angry at Tom, quite angry at all the Langlois-Lefroys! (though I continued to love Mrs. Lefroy until the day she died, and she did try to make it up to me by introducing me to Mr. Blackall, with whom I shared a feeling of indifference).

But I must try to believe it 'was all for the best' so I shall now try to convince myself. You know from my characters of high society that they are for the most part insufferable, with a poverty of ideas. With a husband in Parliament I would have to entertain these boring creatures. At my table would sit some of the most stupid people in England. And - why would I want to be a neighbour of Miss Edgeworth in Longford, when she would not love my *Emma*?

I have now convinced myself of my great unhappiness had I married my Irish friend. I hope you are convinced as well. I am too overcome to go downstairs. I shall pretend illness and hope they will send a tray upstairs, for I am never too unhappy to *eat*. In fact, I could devour an entire chocolate cake with a vanilla cream filling, if I could get my hands on one.

I will finish by saying that I *am* happy for Mr. Lefroy, and I wish

68

him well for the remainder of his life. I wonder if he has ever thought of me, and whether he has or will ever hear of my Darling Children, or read them. *More later -*

11pm

Dear Cassandra

The evening is a little cold, and I never wanted a fire in my room more, not for heat, but for the company of its red glow and crackling wood. I wished to sit beside it in my dressing gown and poke and mope to my heart's content. But I went downstairs after all. I tried to exert myself at dinner for the sake of the company, and I can assure you I did great justice to the apple pie with Ice Cream.

I declined any amusement and went upstairs again with the intention of writing this letter and going to bed early. I had just begun, when I heard a step upon the stairs, a knock on the door, and Miss Edgeworth's asking permission to enter.

And in she came. I rose to greet her and bade her sit upon the only chair, while I sat on the bed. She admired my room, said that hers was painted apple green, which she liked very well, but had thin curtains, which she did not like at all, as she had to get into a corner of the room to undress, well out of sight.

'Are you well?' she asked me. 'You were just beginning a letter; I am sorry if I interrupted you.'

'It is not an interruption,' I told her, indeed glad to see her. She is not you, but I am in dire need of a sister, and having left you behind, she will have to do.

I owned to being a little unwell, and then asked, with an abruptness of manner that must have surprised her, if she knew of a place in Longford named Carrigglass.

'I do,' she said. 'It is the home of the Honourable Sir Thomas Newcomen. There is – or was – a family connection with the Edgeworths a few generations ago. There is an interesting story about Sir Thomas' mother, Miss Charlotte Newcomen. She was an heiress, and in the 1750's almost a victim of an Abduction Club. She was apprehended in the middle of Longford Town by a gentleman fortune-hunter, but she fought him off with great bravery and purpose of mind. A poor old woman came to her assistance, and a Mr. Webster shot the Abductor, and afterwards Miss Newcomen married the man of her choice…a William Gleadowe, but he took her name upon inheriting – so that is why Sir William is a Newcomen – but all of that is neither here nor there, just an interesting history associated with Carrigglass. But why do you enquire of the place?'

The documents had been lying on the bed, and I took them up and gave them to her, for I felt too out of spirits to explain all. She read in silence, just giving a little inhalation now and then, and when she had finished, gave them back to me.

'And this Judge Lefroy – you were acquainted with him?'

'Have you ever been in love, Miss Edgeworth?' I asked her, with an impetuousness that surprised myself.

Her countenance became a little flushed, and she smiled.

'Yes, but not enough.'

She told me that when she was in Paris with her father in 1802, she had had an offer from a Swedish Count, a Mr. Edelcrantz, and had refused him because she would miss Ireland too much, and thought she would not fit into the Swedish Court, where the Count held a prestigious post. But then she paused, looking at me with the expectancy of hearing something very interesting from *me*.

I then told her the full history of my Irish Friend.

Miss Edgeworth got up and walked about the small room, pacing to the window, and looking out, and coming back, and sitting down, and looked lost in abstraction. She seemed to be in deep and rapid thought, her lips pursed a little, her eyes narrowing, then raised to the ceiling for inspiration, until with a sudden: 'May I?' she picked up the documents again and read through them.

All this time I was wishing for a glass of wine, a good Constantia perhaps. But though the tea was available to all, the wine was locked up after dinner. I conceived the idea that later, when everyone was asleep, I would go downstairs and make myself a cup of hot tea, and drink it alone in the kitchen.

Miss Edgeworth sat again. 'Miss Austen,' she began. 'Do you think that a writer writes herself into her work?'

'Yes, I have no doubt of that, whether she means to or not. Are you trying to make out my character from my works?' I asked, smiling.

'In a way, Miss Austen! I wish to pose a question to you. If Judge Lefroy made the acquaintance of the Bennet family of Longbourne, would Elizabeth like him? She has a very independent mind; she breaks the rules, is not overly pious - not pious at all! Imagine a conversation about a subject very important to him - Catholic Emancipation - imagine this very subject at the Bennett dinner table. Judge Lefroy might say - "I do not agree that the Catholics of Ireland – (*that, Miss Austen, is 95% of the population*) should be allowed to make laws, or sit in judgement, and furthermore it is my opinion that every Catholic household should continue to pay tithes to the Protestant clergy." What would Elizabeth Bennett think of his position? You see I think that Lizzy would be quick to tell him that he is being unjust!

'And I think, Miss Austen, that there is a great deal of Elizabeth Bennett in *you*.'

 I pause to absorb the compliment, for a happy compliment it is, before bringing myself back to the question. 'Surely Mr. Lefroy's opposition to giving Catholics a voice in Parliament is not surprising, given that his family was driven from France owing to persecution by Catholics!' But I say it rather slowly, as if to convince myself. It had been well over two hundred years before he was born.

Miss Edgeworth spoke again. 'I am Protestant, as you know – I could not be otherwise so privileged in this country – and we suffered during the '98 Rebellion. We had to remove from our home to a safer house in town. So I understand the Protestant fears and yet I am *for* Catholic Emancipation. I see no evil in it.'

'May I call you Jane?' she asked after I was silent.

After a pause - 'Of course.'

'And please call me Maria. Jane, I do not know your feelings on these subjects. Perhaps you are not of the same mind as I. Our laws against Catholics have, since 1690, caused unbearable wretchedness and poverty. Thankfully, many have been repealed by now.

'I have said too much, perhaps. Forgive me – will you come down for tea? I shall bring you up a cup, if you like. It will not be any trouble.'

'I thank you – I would like that.' I said. I felt a headache; tea would be welcome.

'I have Snickers bars,' she said with a little conspiracy, as if it were sinful. I laughed, and shook my head.

Before she went, she said: 'Poor Newcomen! *Quel Malheur!* His Bank quite a failure! I hope I do not remember this when I next meet him in Real Time.'

While waiting for the tea, I pondered what Miss Edgeworth – Maria – had said.

I might have tempered Tom's opinions, of course, but it is a grave mistake to marry a man in hopes of changing him. No, I would have had to support him in all his views and become his second self. Impossible. You know I do not take up the opinions of our menfolk, who always claim more knowledge and authority. Though James and our other brothers are great Hanoverians[6], I have always sympathized with Mary Queen of the Scots, and as I wrote with passion in my little *History of England* a long time ago, I was then - and still am - partial to the Roman Catholic religion. It is very possible that my Irish Friend and I might not have had a meeting of minds about this. Imagine the dinner conversations in his home, with his political friends, about how to keep the Catholics in check. How could I stand it?

A terrible idea occurs to me - I can imagine my *Mr. Collins* being very much against Catholic Emancipation. Of course his opinion would depend upon that of Lady Catherine de Bourgh, and she

---

[6] Supporters of the Hanover line of Kings, Protestant.

certainly would not favour Roman Catholics being given any powers. She has *no* liberality. Both would be among Mr. Lefroy's most loyal supporters. Oh, what a thought! I will banish it without delay! There, it is *gone*.

Maria brought the tea, and did not refer to the matter, but said that she had this morning obtained a copy of *Jane Eyre*, and she could read it out to me, if I liked. She had walked out and been unable to pass O'Mahony's Bookshop one more time, so she went in and asked about books by the Brontës. The assistant knew immediately of what she spoke and directed her. *Wuthering Heights* was on the shelf also, and others by the Brontës, but these she did not look at – she saw also Mr. Thackeray's *Vanity Fair*. Did she see mine? She did not say – I did not ask. .

I did like to hear *Jane Eyre*. It was very well written, and engaged my interest from the first words, but may have too much gloom for my taste.

Yours affectionately, Jane

Friday Sept 23rd Early Morning

Dear Cassandra

It is wet and windy and dark outside, not at all an appealing day before us, weather-wise. And I have not slept yet.

My clandestine cup of tea during the night did not do me any good. I crept downstairs at two, let myself into the kitchen quietly, and flicked the switch just inside the door, flooding the room with light. It is very glaring at first, and is as bright as a summer day.

I filled the tea kettle and 'plugged it in', found the tea-bags (I forgot to tell you of tea-bags!) and dropped one into a mug -an ugly blue tankard with the words '*Keep Calm and Drink Tea*'). In went the scalding liquid, and to get the milk I only had to open the humming 'fridge.' A light goes on when the door opens. Somebody thought of everything. The door snaps itself shut. Oh the wonders of this time. I helped myself to a biscuit from a crackling paper (everything comes wrapped in papers or a thin transparent film you have to tear at with your nails to open, and when we asked why, Mary said it was because of the Lawyers) – to get back to my story, I sat myself at the table where I could look out the window, at nothing, for there is only a dark wall below the railing on the street.

I was pondering the irony of Mr. Lefroy's George's Street now being named after his arch-rival, Mr. O'Connell, when the door opened behind me. I turned to see Miss Brontë. The surprise of seeing me showed itself in her expression in the first moment, as perhaps it did in mine.

'Oh Miss Austen! I did not know you were up. You too have found out the pleasure of making oneself a cup of tea while the house sleeps!'

I agreed that it was a pleasure indeed, and she bustled about without a pause, reboiling the kettle, unclasping the tea caddy, unwrapping the biscuits.

'Oh, you have the blue mug,' she said, after a pause during which she had looked in the cupboard.

'It is the one you are accustomed to using?' I asked.

'Yes, but never mind. This one will do as well.' She took out a smaller one with a picture on it.

We sat at the kitchen table, not really wishing to talk to each other, but forced by the circumstance. I find Miss Brontë reserved. Neither she nor her sister have much wit or humour.

'Miss Austen, I read your *'Pride and Prejudice'* she said abruptly.

'You read it!' I echoed.

'Yes, this year, 1848, I read it for the first time.'

'What do you think of it?' I asked with eagerness, feeling I was flinging myself under a Coach and Four, but unable to stop myself.

'Oh, Miss Austen, I hope you do not mind some criticism. I mean well. I find that your work wants *passion*. There is nothing of what throbs fast, what throbs full, what the blood rushes through. '

I was silent, but held her eyes with expectation.

'There is too much of the *drawing-room* about it. It is like a well-tended flowerbed, very safe, very elegant, enclosed by a tidy pale. No open country, no fresh air, no blue hill, no bonny beck.'

I was quite taken aback. When I recovered, I said:

'All my novels so far are set too far away from the border to have a bonny anything among them. You have the advantage; you can make all the bonny you wish in Yorkshire.' I smiled.

'You know what I mean!' she cried.

'No open country, no fresh air?' I went on, a little wickedly. 'Lizzy Bennett got her petticoat dirty jumping over a stile. And as to passion, do you think Mr. Darcy should have shot himself after she refused him? That would leave me with quite a dilemma as to who to marry her off to, for Miss Lucas had been very quick to

76

take Mr. Collins when she thought Lizzy didn't want him – '

She looked at me as if I was from Timbuctoo.

'I cannot give you my opinion of *your* work.' I said, wishing to throw the subject away from my child. 'I have not had the opportunity of - reading your book. Please tell me about *Jane Eyre*?' I enquired in a warmer tone, my appetite whetted by the chapter we read. I do not wish to tell her that Maria has procured a copy.

'She is a governess who falls in love with her employer, a Mr. Rochester.'

'Rochester. That is a strong name.' (I might purloin it. Lady Rochester, dowager of Nethermeadow, who holds the fortunes of three fawning nephews in her hands).

'Thank you. Jane Eyre is orphaned, very poor and plain. But her feelings run very deeply, and she is completely miserable.'

'As she should be, in those circumstances.'

'Utterly and completely, because she thinks he does not love her.'

'Why?'

'Because she thinks him in love with another woman, and because she feels so inferior and ill-favoured. But Mr. Rochester is in love with her, and they go to the church to be married, where she finds out he is married already, to the mad woman in the attic.'

'A Gothick romance, then?'

'Oh no! It is a great deal more! There is not much of *melodrama*, I can assure you – only *passion*.'

I have irritated her!

'Miss Austen, may I give you a little advice?'

'I pray do not exert yourself. I will not remember it, you know, in the Real Time morning.' I was being a little discourteous, but her not liking my light and sparkling Darling Child felt unforgiveable.

But Miss Brontë would not be stopped. 'But I want to encourage you, Miss Austen. I would advise you to make your characters throb with life - with unrequited love - blood pulsing quickly through their veins - passions unfulfilled - make them scream out loud on a clifftop into a gale force wind - make them gouge the walls of their prisons with fingernails broken from hard labour - make them suffer and die of love, set them on fire! Drown them until they have only a whimper of breath left!'

'You have not read *Sense and Sensibility*,' I said to her. 'That was my first published book, five years ago. And I am selling very well since; I am indeed very content!'

There was a pause. I spoke again.

'Miss Brontë, perhaps we are not writing the same kind of book.'

She looked at me, not understanding, and took a sip from her mug.

'If you mean that I cannot be amusing and witty, that is completely without foundation. Mr. Rochester is a very clever speaker; he uses a great deal of wit with Jane.'

'I am not in a position to decide whether you can write amusing and witty! But Mr. Rochester - he is handsome as well?'

'Not at all.'

'He needs something to recommend him to Miss Eyre, then. 'I said with more wickedness. 'I suppose he is rich?'

'You are always looking at money! Mr. Rochester is not as rich as Mr. Darcy. The house burns down; he may be made poor by that. And he is blind – there is no harm in my telling you the end; I know you will never read 'Jane Eyre' – they marry.'

'How are you so sure I will never read *Jane Eyre*?'

I thought she flushed a little, and looked away, but then she said: 'Because you are prepared to dislike it so much.'

'Readers have told me that they find my characters entertaining. I would think they are very well-drawn. As for your opinion about my being concerned with money; in a country neighbourhood people talk of money a great deal, as well as keeping an eye out for attachments between the young people, speculating upon fortunes and the lack of. People gossip about each others' health, about newcomers, visitors – about news garnered on morning calls, or upon a walk, or the Assembly Rooms - and news about the family who is first in the district is the most popular news of all. Births, marriages, deaths are all topics for conversation - does the village of Haworth not gossip of these matters?' I asked with genuine surprise.

She looked at me for a moment, but ignored my question, and went on:

'But *I* cannot see, Miss Austen, how your characters will endure at all, unless you give them more passion! Fervor, Ardour, is Everything, Miss Austen!'

'My characters are popular as they are,' I replied with calmness. She glowered again. She is determined to dislike my Lizzies and

Henrys, and perhaps she cannot relate to the warm sociability and the rules that govern them, in my work, due to – what?

'Your readers prefer the lighter kind of book; the kind that does not make them feel much,' she said then. 'your readers like to go calmly to sleep; mine want to throb with joy or sorrow.'

I sighed to myself and found I had no reply to Miss Brontë, for we seem not to speak the same language. Maria Edgeworth does not think much of my works; Charlotte Brontë thinks my characters will not endure! So in two hundred years, Lizzy Bennett will be forgot, and Jane Eyre remembered? I have said that I paint on a bit of ivory, a few inches long, with a fine brush. Are my paintings destined to fade for lack of wild and impassioned fury?

Miss Brontë spoke again, quietly.

'The trouble is, Miss Austen, is that you have not *suffered*. Great Art is the harvest of deep deprivation, the deepest agony.'

She said this in a low voice, acutely conscious of her unique experience, and that of her family, of which I have learned some. Mr. Thackeray has hinted strongly of their history and of present troubles. I was able to abandon my hurt pride and sympathize in her sorrow, for her attitude bespoke a genuine distress, and I thought that there was more upon her mind, more preying upon her, due to her *present* life. Two older sisters died at school (the horrors of schools! You and I and our cousin also know that).

It appears that their mother died young, and that the children have been brought up in a poor, isolated part of Yorkshire with no society. They were left largely to themselves to invent games and worlds of their own. They have but one brother, and great sums were spent on his education, but it appears he is very unwell – a sickness brought on perhaps by himself, by his intemperate habits

- he keeps to his bed, and is not expected to live long. And Emily is – well, Emily. There was a heated argument between them last night. Emily has rescued a stray kitten from a piece of waste ground not far from here. She keeps it in their room, hides it from Anna, and tends it. Her health must be a constant worry. I thought it was best to leave the subject, and she evidently thought so too, for her next sentence was:

'Emily has taught herself how to google.'

'How to – what?'

'Google! How to use the laptop! She entered *'Jane Eyre'* and got eleven million results! My book is extremely popular still. And hers, *'Wuthering Heights'* also – three and a half million hits. There have been plays made from both, and films for television.' And the Big Screen. I am not sure what that means. If you like, Miss Austen, we can google *'Pride & Prejudice'*. Emily is at this moment at the laptop in the little office at the back of the house; she uses it every night. I am going to her now, but first I am going to unplug the kettle, unless you would like more tea?'

I declined. She bade me good night and left. She had left her mug on the table. All drinking mugs have an ugliness but this is saved from that fate by a pretty portrait of a Bride and Groom, just their heads, he a very handsome man in a fine cravat, she beautiful, dark-haired, laughing. The caption says: *P&P 1995.* I hope 'Patrick and Patricia' or 'Peter and Phoebe' have a very happy marriage.

I do not think I want to 'google' *Pride & Prejudice.* How many 'hits' would it get? A thousand?

I must get some sleep, Cass, for I have written directly after coming upstairs. The street outside is very quiet at this time. The

81

trains do not begin to run for another hour or so.

Yours affectionately, Jane

Dear Cassandra

You see before you a more cheerful Jane, who thinks that she and Tom would have been very happy, as she would have steered him in all of the right directions, and he would have been receptive to all of her ideas. But this conviction may only last a while, I have already had it three times, and then its very opposite, and I do not know which way I shall swing by the end of the letter.

We are not to go to Longford after all; Miss E is now afraid of its being too altered, and being very disappointed. But we are not to be disillusioned, and a better scheme is in place. We will visit a Great House hereabouts, one which is open to the Publick. We think Dromoland Castle or Adare Manor. Both are Inns now - but of a very luxurious kind, and we can stroll about the Parks as we wish. I think Dromoland Castle, the former seat of the O'Briens, sounds the more interesting of the two.

I have to confess an interest in this Laptop business, and surprisingly, Emily is captivated and has now begun to fiddle during the daytime also. She should do no such thing of course, but Emily, when she is interested in something, must have her way. She has played with the 'keyboard' and is close to mastering it. Miss Brontë attends her in this, standing over her, and offers suggestions – 'Try this! Click on that!'

Gina had a call this morning on her I-phone, and walked about the hall with it, and then outside, and was very agitated

82

afterwards, so I took the opportunity to ask her what the matter was. She said that a friend in America has told her that her *'ex-boyfriend is dating another girl'*. I asked her if she still loved him, and she said that she did, and wiped tears from her dark eyes - then I tactfully broached the subject of Doug, and she replied that Doug was a cheater, and was out to ruin her ex-boyfriend...I wondered if I should tell her that Doug had stated something to the contrary, but thought it better not to. Poor Gina! She showed me a likeness of Rowland Hatton– for it is he - upon her I-phone. He is a fair-haired, good-looking man, not as handsome as Doug. There is a reserve about his eyes. I wish to find out more, but must bide my time.

I must leave off for now – we are having *pitza* (spelling?) for lunch. Gina prepared it (keeping her word in spite of her broken heart, good girl -) It is a favourite dish of the Italians, and Gina is Italian-American. She assured us that we will love it; a baked white crust with tomato paste and melted cheese on top, with bits of bacon and perhaps other 'toppings'. Do I make you envious? I hope so. Then we are to go out in the Car. This is the first time!

Later: We returned a little while ago, after an enjoyable afternoon, with new experiences and new learning. The car – which Eric says is not a car but an aptly-named People-Carrier is completely enclosed, has three rows of front facing seats, and a funny bobble-thing hanging from a mirror in the front which seems to have no function except to amuse. The driver sits in the front right seat. He has at his disposal a wheel something like a ship's wheel, and an array of lights and controuls, which he operates with equanimity while talking without ceasing. He offered one of us to ride in front with him, and I being the most courageous, took the seat with an alacrity that would do justice to Julia Bertram and her hopes, only Eric is no Frank Crawford, being old, fat and married. Mr. Thackeray happily did not accompany us, preferring to plan his

83

own tours, (he walked to the Railway Station to take a train to Cork) so I did not feel I had to give way to him for the preferred 'passenger seat'. He has been in the car before, in any case, as he took a drive from Eric to the shop the other even, and I do not think he liked it much. Gina did not accompany us either. She had to go to India, where it is night, to fill up a tour for the Silk Road.

And so, belted into our seats (it is the law) we set off, rolling down the street, turning a corner, stopping and starting at intervals, obeying a complicated set of road rules which every driver must pass an official test on before obtaining a license. Then over the Shannon bridge, and we left the city behind us.

Maria begged Eric not to go so fast, and he chuckled: 'You ain't seen nothing yet, I'm putting the foot down.' And so that is what I assume he did, for we began to go very rapidly indeed on a wide road, so that the hedges whizzed by in a blur…then – Emily cried out:

'Oh, a horse! A horse!' She had seen one of the creatures, and yes, in a few minutes she saw another in a field, and several more, and a few donkeys into the bargain. The dear animals! How we feasted our eyes upon the blurs!

A fine old medieval Castle named Bunratty greeted us next, but we did not stop, though a street of fine shops caught our interest.

Then a loud, loud noise – I have heard the like before, but not found out what might be the cause – and I saw a sight that almost made my stomach turn – a large silvery bird-like object crossing the sky almost directly in front of us. It had a tail sticking up upon which was emblazoned a colourful sign – I know not what. There were gasps from the rear seats.

'Relax, ladies, it's only an aeroplane,' said Eric. 'You didn't

84

believe me when I told you what those white streaks in the sky were. Well, there you are, an aeroplane now making its descent into Shannon Airport.'

It was true; our eyes catching a glint of metal one day at the head of a white plume stretching behind it in the sky, he had told us that there were People up there, being transported from one country to another. We were sure that he had been quizzing us.[7] I know you will not believe me, Cassandra; I find it next to impossible to believe that people can fly. Now I know I am dreaming.

But Miss Brontë believes it. Moreover, she declared then she would like to go up in an aeroplane instead of visiting an old House, where there would be little of novelty, but Eric said it would not be possible to do that, and I was relieved. Our eyes followed the silver object as it descended lower and lower and disappeared behind some trees. It took all of a few moments.

But to the object of our journey – Dromoland Castle. It has fallen now into the hands of Americans, who run it as a Hotel, and the present Lord Inchiquin lives in a modest home in a nearby town, doing for himself, Eric says.

We were mighty pleased to turn in a grand gate and drive up an avenue to a Great House. We were surrounded by extensive parklands gently sloping towards a fine lake ringed by a path with extensive woods behind. We saw a herd of deer, and our distant view took in two rivers. Eric 'parked' the car and we got out to a fresh breeze and a walking tour about the grounds. There was a row of neat cottages placed near the west wing…how I would like to place one of my Families in this Estate! Who would they be? Fitzgeralds, perhaps. Two unmarried daughters, one a

---

[7] Teasing

snobbish girl, the other sweet and mild, but with a knowledge of her own heart…her admirer almost attached to the elder, but hesitating…*she* is in love with the clergyman, and her family are opposed…'you get my drift' as Gina says. But back to Dromoland…

The Castle had a Gothick appearance, but it dates from the middle of the nineteenth century. The staircase to the front entrance was very grand indeed, and the Great Hall, though functioning as an office where guests register to stay, had all of the ambience of a stately room. Eric boldly led us to the Bar. The Bar! Where men drink! But there were women there also, and he ordered 'drinks'. I have visited Great Houses in England, but they were private homes and we did not sit down to eat or drink. I boldly ordered a glass of wine. We are all impressed with the place, though Maria Edgeworth has been to so many fine places in London and Paris, that this house, though beautiful, affected her in no particular way. What struck her, and all of us, is that no Family lived there, and there were no tenants, no farmers who pay rent, no village or villagers who belonged to the Estate.

This was a matter of great concern to Maria, and she asked Eric on the way home – 'If all of the landlords are gone – who looks after the Poor? Do not tell me that there are no Poor. In spite of the prosperity we see, there must be poor people, there will always be poor people. Old people, orphans, cripples of mind and body - who looks after them if the landlords are gone? For I cannot see that a Parish, without the support of the landlords, can do it all.'

Eric replied that the Government has charge of them, and further explained that everybody pays taxes enough to look after their health and welfare. I admire Maria's concern, this question seems to occupy her greatly, and I would think that her father's tenants must be secure and happy.

When we returned to the house, Gina was back. She was pacing up and down, holding her phone in one hand and talking into it, and holding a tin-can of Coca-Cola – a black lemonade - in the other. (I have often seen her walk by munching and sipping when it is nowhere near a mealtime. The people now eat and drink whenever they feel like it, and are never, I suppose, avidly looking forward to their meals as a result).

'What am I supposed to do now? I mean, this is the last thing I expected. I thought this Organization was secure when I joined. Everything was in good shape. I mean Fortune 500 good shape. If there's a merger, what's going to happen to me? And Rena? Why didn't they tell us? They never tell us anything! At the last meeting, they said we were doing really well. Yeah, I know, they didn't want to tell us the truth. Nobody wants to tell us the truth. What's *RelativityExperience* like to work for anyway? I'm scared they'll consolidate our jobs, and you know, first in, first out. Ok, goodbye. Keep me informed. Ok.'

I have no idea what she is talking of. When Eric handed her the bill from Dromoland Castle Bar, she cried out:

'Eric! They will go crazy when I send this one in. It's totally not on budget to take people to expensive places. Wine at €30 a glass! Why didn't you take them for a Big Mac? That would be a real 2016 cultural experience. Eric, they won't reimburse you for this. We are going through a merger and we are pretending to be viable. I don't even dare send it in, for goodness sake!'

'The taste of a good wine lingers long after the price is forgotten.' Eric said with a flourish.

'Are you crazy or what? They're not even going to remember this! Eric! Burger King next time! Kentucky Fry!' Gina took a long gulp from the tin-can.

I will sleep well tonight, for I am excessively tired. The exercise and the air did me a great deal of good. Miss Brontë and I are cordial; she is at least honest as to her opinion about *P&P*. I am not as offended as you must think I am; upon reflection I far prefer *her* review to Madame de Staël's dismissive *'vulgaire'*.[8] No doubt if she had attended the Meryton Assembly, she would have concurred with the Bingley sisters in their views. It would of course please me if Authors of note praised my work, but I will be content with my readers - the Miss Smiths *and* a Prince Regent or two. At least I have the *Quarterly Review* writing in my favour, would I knew who the writer was; I cannot find out.[9]

Yrs affect.

Jane

September 24th Saturday

Dear Cassandra

This morning I came downstairs to the sound of an irritated Eric on the phone. 'But I charge it every day – every morning it's dead. I expect better life from something I paid one hundred and twenty euros for – all right – I'll bring it in later. Goodbye'. He hung up the phone (Homes are full of phones. They hang upon the wall; they sit upon desks and tables; they ride in pockets. There is one beside my bed. One cannot be without this instant means of communication.)

---

[8] Madame de Staël was a Swiss author. She was an aristocrat and well-travelled, and very celebrated in the literary salons of Europe.
[9] It was later speculated to have been Sir Walter Scott.

'Good Morning, Jane!'

'Good morning!' I responded. 'Eric – may I please ask a favour?'

'Of course!'

'When you are next using your laptop, could you - google something for me?'

'Google! Where did you hear the word?' He paused, but I am not about to tell him of Emily using his laptop. 'Of course, Jane! Say the word! Or words! But I have to buy a new Battery. It's kaput. Dead as a doornail.'

'Battery?'

'Yes, what runs it…the power - '

'Electricity?' I say with eagerness.

'Exactly! It's using too much power – er – electricity.'

'Oh, Eric…tomorrow is Sunday, when is Divine Service?'

'Oh, Divine Service! Let me see…if ye're Church of England, I expect ye'll all want to go to St. Mary's Cathedral. I will check the times.'

Eric did not use his laptop all day. Instead he went to his shop, and invited us there for a visit, where we joined him about eleven o'clock, and picked our way through his collection of Antiques, many of which were inventions new to us, though I did see a dinner set like the purple lozenge Edward bought in the Wedgewood shop, and Maria could have sworn that one of the old oil paintings used to hang in a neighbour's home.

And back to our lodgings for lunch, where Gina was in a state of great distress, because she had gotten a 'text' – a short message – from her friend in Time Travel Tours, saying that she had seen her name on a list of people to be 'laid off'. She will lose her place. Poor Gina! She is unfortunate indeed!

'It's so unfair!' she wept. 'How am I going to pay my rent? And my mom's medical bills are due. I'm still paying off for my car!'

(Remember Gina's home is in America – New York to be exact. Perhaps the Government does not help the poor there.)

Maria said: 'My dear, go to your Employer, explain the situation, and I am sure, that if he is a decent man, he will offer you some Relief, or even another place. He surely cannot dismiss you in such a manner, if he has been pleased with your work, and knows your circumstances. Appeal to his sense of duty, to his Christian heart.'

'Who, the C.E.O.? I don't even know him.'

Miss Brontë asked what a C.E.O. was, and Gina replied that it was a Chief Executive Officer – the Top Dog, the Head Honcho. The Guy who runs the company.

'What! You do not know him? Does he not tour his Estate – or offices – or whatever it is he is Top Dog of?' exclaimed Maria.

'I know his name; oh and what he looks like from photos. He's called Frederick Crump. He certainly doesn't know who I am. Touring the branches? No, he shows up in Headquarters for a Board Meeting once a month, and the rest of the time he's on his yacht in Florida.' There followed a misunderstanding, with Maria asking why he hunted pirates, and it was established that a yacht is now used for the purposes of pleasure, not pursuit.

'Oh, in any case, he is an *Absentee*.' she said with aggravation. 'the

90

very worst kind. The man who does not trouble to know the people whose welfare God has placed under his particular care. A very bad kind of man; I see human nature has not altered on that score. In our day, it is the Landlord of an Estate, today, it is the C.E.O. If he does not see the people who are dependent upon him, cannot put a name with a face, he cannot care about them.'

'I bet he is getting a humungous Bonus for bringing about this merger, too,' Gina said darkly. 'He and his Executive Team are getting richer, but they are laying workers off.'

'When will this - layoff happen?' I asked Gina.

'I don't know. And – that's another thing, Jane. With this merger, TTT will be gone. You will be the guests of *RelativityExperience*. I don't know what exactly will change for you; I think they do some things cheaper, and you'll only get a continental breakfast. You know, cereal, coffee or tea, rolls and marmalade, that kind of thing.'

'I think we shall bear the loss very well. It will be nothing, compared to what you and your friends must face. What about Rena? Will she still have a situation?'

'Rena will probably be ok for now; they need the Directors to keep the ship afloat during the merger. After the merger they start looking at consolidating senior positions. Rena will be in some danger then. In a merger, you never know. You can just show up to work one morning and be told to pack up and go.'

We pondered the inhumanity of this. In an age with so many advances, so many marvels, greed and avarice are as popular as ever.

'Is Doug in jeopardy?' I asked.

'Doug? I doubt it. Doug is very good at taking care of Doug.'
Gina's tone was bitter.

'Are you sure, Gina? Perhaps you misunderstand Doug.'

She stared at me, her dark eyes large with surprise.

'Oh, Jane, not you as well,' she said, in an almost despairing
fashion.

'What do you mean?'

'He got to you too.'

'Got to me?' She did not have to tell me what the phrase meant. I
began to wonder why she felt such dislike of Doug, this man who
had so impressed me. Was I mistaken in my impressions?

'He talked to you, didn't he? Bad-mouthed Rowland, and said he
wanted to save me from him.'

'So – you are saying, Gina, that Doug is the – Jerk?'

She laughed. 'Doug called Rowland a Jerk, right? Yeah, Doug's
the jerk. He's my co-worker I told you about who exceeded his
Quota by lying to the housemaid - '

Her phone rang again (a little tune, repeats over and over) and she
apologized that she had to take the call, it was about a guest on
SilkRoad16th, and that she would tell me about Rowland soon.

I pondered her words – Doug is very good at taking care of Doug.
Was he, perhaps, a Mr. Wickham? Charming, with pleasing
manners, but self-serving? How he duped that poor maid. I
conclude that I was very deceived in Doug Shaw. Poor Gina – she
is in a grave situation. A broken heart, and facing hardship - if I

could write her out of this and into happiness, I would...
Yrs affect., JA

Dear Cass

Are you missing me yet? You must have turned over twice by now. I have been in Church and said my prayers, and you have slept.

St. Mary's Cathedral is a fine building on a hill overlooking the main streets of the city and river. Part of the interior is devoted to the exhibition of ancient articles, and many side-altars are fitted-up as to be of great historical interest to a visitor. It has a good-sized park, and the service, I was pleased to see, had some hymns that are familiar to us in our time. But I was dismayed to see so few people attend. Have people forgotten the comfort religion can be in their lives? For though people seem to own a great deal of things now, I doubt if ownership of goods has caused suffering and hardship to cease. That will always be part of life. Everybody stared at our hats and gloves. (I forgot to mention that we did procure them, and it was not easy to get a nice hat – if we could have got our hands on some willow, we would have made our own bonnets!)

After the Service we walked about the cathedral yard, and I quite by accident almost fell over a Headstone - 'Lefroy'. It is that of his parents. It made my Irish friend present to me in a way, to see this so close – and know that he must have stood here in this spot during the last, sad ceremonies and mourned.

But I am no Harriet Smith, to cry over my love forever, until I meet the next, which I have never done, so I will just cry over the fact that this morning, Mary was very cross with Eric, for she only now found out about Dromoland Castle, and was very upset that she was not of the party. It seems that day of the week is her *Zumba* Class, and Eric was of the persuasion that she would not give it up for anything, and therefore never mentioned it to her. She reminded him that she it was who was expected to take us to Longford, to see some God-forsaken bogs, (thankfully Maria was not by to hear this) but that when they were to go to a fine Hotel that has the best wine-list in Ireland, she was to be left out of it. She had never, ever been to anyplace like it, and whenever they went out, it was always to Bobby Byrnes. Eric wanted to know what was wrong with Bobby Byrnes. She always seemed to like it before.

Mary went on to say that with the merger, if the new Company did not pay them as well as TTT, that she was not going to run the Guest House anymore. She was going to get a job where she was appreciated – she could get a job in an office no bother. Nine to Five Monday to Friday. She had her Sales Manager skills; she had Advanced Spreadsheets. She had been assured that Time Travellers would be easier than modern tourists; she wasn't so sure about that now. Twice she had been kept waiting while Maria dressed for dinner. Did Miss Edgeworth think she had come to Downton Abbey? And you had to explain everything to them. Emily Brontë hadn't eaten a thing she had cooked. Nothing. She was at her wits end about Emily.

Cass, you will think me dreadful to have listened to all this – I was a veritable Miss Steele, listening at the door. But I was not at the door, I was halfway upstairs, and yes, perhaps I ascended a little more slowly than I should have. I felt sorry for Eric at first, but then my sympathy faded – he was willing to take us to Dromoland Castle but did not wish to take us to 'the Bog' –you can be sure when anything unpleasant is afoot, a man is sure to get himself out of it. I said as much to Maria, and she was dying of laughter, though I tactfully left out the 'Bog' allusion. We are grown quite friendly, and chat more easily.

We were taken by hackney cab (remember do not see Horses!) to an Inn – the Green Hills Hotel a short distance from the City – for Sunday Dinner! We queued up with trays, and were handed plates of thick slices of roast beef with lashings of brown gravy, golden roast potatoes, fried onions and mushrooms and creamed carrots. We then carried the trays ourselves to a table. We ate heartily, all of us, except Emily. Emily just picked at hers. Mr. Thackeray, who feels the lack of male company, left us after dessert and coffee to take his daily ramble. So it was just the females, and Maria broached the subject of Gina's dilemma in being without employment. Gina, however, brushed this subject aside, and began to talk of her *heart* with an intimacy that was surprising given that she has not known us for long.

'I said I would tell you about Rowland,' she began rather loudly, and with some enthusiasm.

The genteel thing to do would have been to have steered her from the disclosure, for she should be saved from her youthful impetuosity in exposing herself. But we greatly wished her to go on, while knowing that our greater wisdom should caution her.

Maria made a gallant effort. 'Such candour is flattering to us, Gina, but there is no necessity, you know, on your part.' she said, very kindly and properly, and not meaning a word of it.

There was a moment of surprised silence from Gina, and Maria realized that she had been taken too seriously.

'I mean, it is such a publick place!' she added in a whisper. 'It occurred to me that you might not wish to speak of a subject of such delicacy, *here*. That is all I meant by my words.'

95

'If I didn't want to talk about it here, would I have brought it up?' demanded Gina. 'But maybe you feel uncomfortable with me talking of my love life.' She sat back and took a draught of coffee. 'I guess, in your Time, it is not a cool thing to do?'

Charlotte cast a glance at Maria that showed her intense provocation, before leaning towards Gina, and saying with emphasis:

'Miss Edgeworth, I am sure, did not mean to give that impression. I wish very much to know of it; perhaps I can be of help. *I have been in love.*' She added, her voice dropping.

'Really?' Gina's eyes widened. 'But you're not with him now? What happened?'

'He was married,' Charlotte said with great gloom, while Emily looked sharply at her.

'What a jerk.' Gina sipped her coffee.

'Oh no,' sighed Charlotte. 'He is an angel, and innocent; I was wrong – but I could not controul my feelings for Professor Heger.'

'Your story sounds a lot more interesting than mine.' Gina said, sitting forward. 'Where did you meet him?'

Emily coughed loudly. 'We shall not speak any more of the Professor,' she said sternly. 'Gina, we shall hear *you*.' Her voice was practically a command, and Gina placed her cup on the table and took a deep breath.

'I met Rowland in Central Park when I was walking my employer's dog, Mitzy, He was walking his mom's dog. The dogs became friends.'

(What an interesting way to meet a young man!)

96

'He was a cute guy, handsome, but a bit distant – shy. One day when our dogs were playing together, we sat on a bench and talked. He had been born in Connecticut and grown up in the Hamptons (that's an upscale district) and now he was a business student at Cornell University. His mom became widowed and moved to Manhattan in the City and he lived in an apartment near Cornell and he visited his mom a few times a week.

'My Dad was a restaurant manager - *Luigi's* on Queen's Boulevard – and one day at work, on a spring day, he just collapsed, and died. He'd never been sick a day in his life and it was a total shock. He was only forty-five. I was eighteen at the time. Mom went to pieces for a while, and she never really recovered her health. She was fired from her job. And there were five of us kids, I was the second eldest, and there was very little money. My older sister lived at home and I moved out to make things easier, and started to work and then two years later I'd saved enough to enroll in community college. I had a few different jobs and one of them was caring for an old lady who lived near Central Park.

'Rowland and I met several times by accident in the Park, or maybe it wasn't an accident – I thought it was funny how he always walked Homer the same time as I walked Mitzi - well then he asked me out and we started dating.'

'We dated for four months. We had a lot in common, we talked about a lot of things, we love the same Art and Museums, and we had the same sense of humour as well. I talk a lot and he – well - Rowland's a listener. He was generous; but he also knew that I didn't want him to pay for everything and that I needed the dignity of paying my way sometimes.' (A dignity indeed, when a woman can offer to pay! And how gracious of a man to accept!)

Gina went on: 'But what I really loved about him was his

97

sincerity. I felt so comfortable with him. Rowland was the real deal. It was great and I began to think he was 'the One'. '

'And then as the months went on, I thought it was time perhaps that he should introduce me to his Mother. But he didn't. I knew she was only a stone's throw away in the Fleetwood Apartment Complex. That's another upscale place. You have movie directors and Broadway people there, stockbrokers and all kinds of rich people.'

'One day, we were supposed to go to a movie, and he said he would pick me up at my apartment – but my mom called me, and she was freaked out about a bill she got from the Electric Company, and she thought they were saying that she owed them a lot of money – my sister was away, visiting a friend – and I knew it had to be an error but I had to go over there right away, so I called Rowland on my way and told him what had happened – I said I didn't think I had to cancel the date but could he pick me up instead at my home in Queens?

'I suppose I was trying to force something. Because I could have just canceled and gone to the movies another night. But I kind of made him come over to my house.

'Queens isn't upscale like the Hamptons or Manhattan; and where we live is right next to a railway line so that the house shakes whenever a train goes by. So Rowland drives up in his Lexus – that's a Luxury car - and I let him in and introduce him to my mom, who has calmed down by now and very happy to see her daughter dating a classy guy like Rowland Hatton. She was very nice to him and then unfortunately my kid sisters looked out the upstairs window and they yelled to their friends across the street: 'Gina's boyfriend owns a fancy car!' My mom yelled at them to shut up and I was mortified. Then the 6:17 from Penn Station went by and the house shook. There was this horrible silence after that.

'We continued to date and he was still the same sweet guy, but he still didn't introduce me to his mother. I mean, she was only three blocks away! Her apartment overlooks the park! She could probably even see us walking from her window! I began to think about *nothing else* but why he wasn't introducing me to his mother and I became convinced he was ashamed of me.'

'Gina,' I asked, 'where does Doug come into the story?'

'I was coming to that - Doug was the son of Mrs. Hatton's best friend. This woman had died and Mrs. Hatton had been very kind to Doug; she liked him a great deal.

'I was in the park one day waiting for Rowland and along comes this guy with Homer; and introduces himself as Doug Shaw. Well the dogs were friends and romped along together so Doug and I walked together too. He told me that Rowland had called his mom and said he couldn't come over and so Mrs. Hatton called him, Doug, to come and walk Homer. Doug implied that this was a common enough thing that Rowland cancelled out on his mom to go shopping or to the Hair Salon and then he would step in and take her. Doug kept on talking about Rowland and it wasn't so much what he said, as what he didn't say – such as, there's a kid sister – seventeen years old - and Rowland is very careful about who she mixes with…he is very controlling of her friendships - and he says Mrs. Hatton confides in him - Doug claimed she says 'I can always depend on *you*, Doug.' He claimed that *he* ran all her errands and did everything for her, fixed things for her and serviced her car. Rowland didn't do any of that, Doug said. He was always too busy, getting his postgraduate degree. He is very ambitious and won't let anything get in his way. He walked his mother's dog; that was all he did for his mom. Doug said all this in a quiet, regretful way, as if he was reluctantly telling me, for my own sake…like he knew I loved Rowland and I needed to know that it wasn't going to come to anything.'

'What sort of – family does Doug come from?' Maria asked.

'Except for his mother, he doesn't really talk of them,' Gina said. 'He has a brother who lives in another State, and I think he has an older sister who is married. He's vague.'

'Oh Gina, Gina!' Maria said with strong reproach. 'Evasiveness is a very bad sign in a man.'

'Oh, I know that now….oh, he also told me that Rowland was expected to marry very well.

'So I began to be certain that Rowland thought I wasn't good enough for him, and that he was only amusing himself with me. Doug continued to talk to me and by the time we had reached the end of our walk, I felt I had found out so much about Rowland from this nice, sweet guy, that I didn't know before. I thought that Rowland felt nothing for me. So when Doug suggested we meet again I said OK. So, after meeting Doug a few times, I texted Rowland that it was over and Doug became my boyfriend'.

This was met with great consternation from her hearers. She sighed from her heart and was the picture of regret, her eyes fixed upon the table. All the time she had been speaking she had been occupying her hands with her red paper napkin, folding it lengthways into little pleats and now, looking at it with a kind of abstraction, during which I was about to think she would make a fan of it by gripping one end and opening the other, she crumpled the whole into a tight ball and threw it upon the dessert plate.

And she said: 'And Rowland did not come after me. Doug was

right – Rowland cared nothing for me. Obviously.'

Another sigh.

'Then I graduated and got this job, and I convinced Rena that Doug could do it too – and she gave Doug a job with TTT. We worked together setting up *AncientKingsBC* and we had a good time, until I found out he was having an affair with Karly in Marketing. Karly is the wife of the Vice President.'

The revelation brought a gasp from all of us.

'So I dumped Doug. Even though he had borrowed money from me and I knew I probably would never get it back; I couldn't stand to be with him anymore. I also had figured out that he was a liar and only out to benefit himself. Then Karly dumped Doug as well. Now Doug wants me back. But I know he doesn't love me; he just wants now what he can't have. He will marry a woman with money. That's the kind of person he is. Doug needs money; I found out he has huge debts - Mrs. Hatton is his only hope of getting any. Rowland stands in his way. I think he'll continue to work on Mrs. Hatton until she prefers him to her own son.'

'Do not go back to Doug!' cried Charlotte Brontë.

'But Karly must have done something for Doug, because he still has a job under the merger agreement. He blackmailed her, I bet. Meantime, I have nothing, and I really regret that I listened to Doug about Rowland. I was such a fool.'

There was a little pause. Then the advice began. Charlotte thought that Gina should write Rowland a very long letter full of the passion of love she felt, leaving nothing of her feelings unstated, and ask him outright if he is ashamed of her. Maria gave the opinion that she should put it all behind her and start again, for she was sure that there were many respectable men about, suitable for Gina, and who would not object to Queens and the trains, and she had learned valuable lessons from both attachments. Emily was applied to for her opinion, but she shrugged her shoulders and said she had none, but when pressed, said that these kinds of misjudgments were irredeemable, and the business was without hope or remedy; there was too much of the most painful sensations, and Rowland, if he loved Gina, would have challenged Doug to a duel; he had not done so, and Gina must draw her own wretched conclusions from his inaction. It was the longest speech that we had ever heard from Emily Brontë, and we wished she had kept silent. I said that Gina, if she paid attention to her own heart, would discover herself what was the best course of action to take, for she had a better guide within herself than any of us in this matter, if she would pay attention to it.

I am sure that Gina should not have 'texted' Rowland to end the attachment. Texting is just a very short written message sent over a phone, often using abbreviations and symbols. It sounded a callous thing to do, and he might have been extremely hurt by it, and when I contrived to meet her on her own later I said as much.

'Do you really think so?' she asked me, plaintively, her dark eyes huge and round.

'Yes, I do think so. I should be very, very cross if I got a text with that news, from a person I loved. What he must have felt!'

'I thought he felt relief that I had done it, and saved *him* the trouble of dumping *me*.'

'You were so plagued about his opinion of your mother and your home that this must have affected your judgment. Just because you contrived to introduce him to your mother does not mean that he should immediately introduce you to his. You should not have tried to force his hand, Gina.'

Gina clapped white and gold sparkling fingertips over her mouth for a moment.

'You are so right, Jane! I became obsessed by what he thought of my home. I assumed and expected that he would give me the cold shoulder, and even when he didn't, I became obsessed with the thought of meeting his mom.'

'He may have had good reasons to delay the introduction. Perhaps he had to win her over to the view that he was entitled to make his own decisions in life. He may not have mentioned this to you, for fear that you would think ill of his mother, who, of course, he would wish you to love.'

'Oh I feel so dumb now! Especially about texting him to dump him. But it is too late now! He may never forgive me.'

But I had not finished what I wished to say, much as it was to affect her.

'Rowland may dislike Doug as much as Doug dislikes him, and knowing Doug's pleasant manners and fashion of winning people to him by his insincere professions of affection, he may have been very hurt indeed by the knowledge that Doug was now preferred over him, and that you were now thinking ill of *him*, and quite unreasonably.'

'Oh Jane, that is so true!'

She ran upstairs in a fever of emotion, and I let myself out the front door for a much-needed solitary walk in the People's Park.

'Dump!' what a word. More tomorrow, I am sure of it – are you dreaming at Chawton? I will wager you that mine is by far the more interesting. But perhaps you are up during the night, and have looked upon me. I pray you do not try to wake me to tell me your Dream, for then you will wonder at my deep slumber and short nose.

Your affect sister
JA

Monday September 26th

Dear Cass

The merger is ongoing, and Doug Shaw has been charged with a special project in which he is in charge of Guest Budgets, and also keeps his other role in Guest Promotion. It is an advancement for him, but he still reports to Rena. He is touring all of the Locations, to see 'where cuts can be made' according to Gina.

And so we had the pleasure of meeting Doug again this morning. He was present at breakfast, asked if this cooked breakfast was the usual fare, and I am afraid he will cut us back to black tea and dry toast from tomorrow. I no longer think him as handsome as I did.

He summoned us to a meeting in the parlour afterwards. Standing in the middle of the floor, he reminded us of our Contract, and how nothing had been asked of us as yet beyond having our photographs taken, but he had a plan. Cassandra, we are to engage in some sort of 'Presentation'.

'Here's my thought,' he said, waving his hands about 'We will hold a Living History Event with an English Literature 19th Century theme. You dress up in costumes true to your Time, and we will introduce you as yourselves. You can give a short presentation about your writing. Everyone will think you are Re-Enactors. You will be the last word in authenticity for your Times and your Works. We will have a reception afterwards, and you can mingle with the crowd, make conversation, and be sociable. I'll work with our Marketing guys to get it filmed for TV.'

We were astounded. But Mr. Thackeray was very pleased with the scheme, and rose from his chair and announced that he was a seasoned lecturer, having toured America speaking of English Humorists. He offered to undertake the Lecture full and complete, thus relieving the Ladies of the burden – this said with a great bow in our direction - but Doug raised his hand, and told him that with respect, Mr. Thackeray, the ladies were not to be relieved of the work, and I would have felt disappointed if Doug had taken Mr. T up on his offer, for I should not liked to have sat by and listened to Mr. Thackeray lecture upon my work.

'So, for you, Thackeray – you can talk of *Vanity Fair*. Jane – *Pride & Prejudice*. Charlotte – *Jane Eyre* of course. Emily, *Wuthering*.

Emily looked at him squarely.

'*I* will not participate.'

He remonstrated with her, until finally she spat: 'I would sooner speak to the dogs in the Park!' and she got up and left the room.

Doug said nothing for a moment, and then said: 'We can refine the details later. Gina, can you try the University for a venue?'

'If this is a success,' he added, 'We can maybe take it on the road. Charlotte, I need you to convince your sister.'

'She will not be convinced, Doug. When Emily has made up her mind about something, there is no changing it. She is a genius, you know.'

'Sure she is. That explains a lot.' Doug used a sarcastic tone. 'Tell her if she doesn't go along with us, she is going to be put on a diet of bread and water, like somebody out of one of the hideous schools you wrote about.'

'I wish she would eat that,' her sister said.

To conclude, Cass, it is all arranged. The date is set for next Saturday. We have to make our Notes, and get our 'Costumes' for our ReEnactor Roles.

Gina must be unhappy about the present situation with Doug. She is forced to be in his company – and he has authority over her! But more later, I am sure, about Gina and Doug – I want to tell you that this afternoon, I could wait no longer to visit a bookshop. I too went to O'Mahonys, and I was not at all sorry about it, for it is a fine place, with three floors, and I browsed there for quite some time. I looked about and found a section labeled 'Fiction,' and I went over there and looked among the 'A's' - and saw nothing! I felt a disappointment surge through me. The Brontës are in print; but I am not....I turned to examine the stock in general, and who did I encounter, only Maria! She was buying another book, and looked so guilty! We have not gone on with *Jane Eyre*, for we are not enough alone to read it, and must, in the evenings, keep company together all of us in the parlour. However, later when I met Maria on the stairs as we were coming down to dinner, she had a surprising admission: - 'I am reading *Persuasion*!' At first I did not know to what she referred, but then it became clear that I have changed the name from '*The Elliots*' to '*Persuasion*'! Indeed you and Henry have advised me so; now you see, you have gotten your way – Maria however went on to say that it was *my best work*. She likes it very well, and said: 'It appears to me, especially in all that relates to poor Anne and her lover, to be exceedingly interesting and natural. The love and the lover admirably well drawn. The first meeting after their long separation is admirably well done. And Captain Wentworth taking the boisterous child from her back as she kneels to tend to the sick boy - I felt myself in Anne's place, felt all the gratitude and tenderness of the act. And the overheard conversation about the nut! But I must stop: I have got no farther than the disaster of Miss Musgrave's jumping off the steps. Do not tell me how it all turns out!'

It is *Musgrove*, not *Musgrave*, but I forgive her – I asked her where she had found a copy, and she said 'O'Mahonys, that was my purpose in going there today.' 'But I looked for my Works – I could not find anything there!' I said. She said that I had been looking in the wrong section – we are not in *Fiction*, but in the *Classics*, which is another area!

Yours most truely. Jane

Later on Monday

Dear Cass

I am indulging you with yet another letter! No doubt you have not slept a wink since the last one, which sits in my drawer. Maria and I had a little conference about Gina, and the great danger she must be in from Doug. He holds power over her, and he may attempt to abuse her for his own personal gratification. We are sure that Gina will resist such a demand, if it were made. But she could then lose her job, and her mother's medical bills would be unpaid – we do not like to think of her mother being in the Debtor's Prison, and are sure that Gina has thought of that as well, and may succumb to Doug to save her mother.

107

Emily did not appear for the remainder of the day, and when she did not come down to dinner time, Mary became very disturbed. Charlotte said she was not ill, just wished to be alone. Mary took her up a tray, to be turned away at the door. After that she declared that Emily would have to see a doctor because she would not be responsible for her. She was 'anorexic'. She had heard of 'anorexics' having heart attacks and dying suddenly. She would not have that happen under her roof; Emily had to see a doctor or else leave the house. Miss Brontë said that Emily would not see any doctor; *that* she was very sure about.

Doug was summoned from his Hotel (Adare Manor, as expensive a place as Dromoland Castle) and heard all of her complaints; he said that Emily was staying, for she had to fulfil her contract. Miss Brontë interjected here, and said that Miss Emily should go home. However, she had a suggestion, and that was the youngest sister, Anne, could replace her. Anne was sociable, and she would be happy to speak and 'mingle', which was what was required in the business. Miss Brontë also said that there was no need to print out another *DuplicYou*; the one for Emily would do for Anne as well.

And so it was simple; Miss Emily was to go home tonight, wake up Anne enough for her to enter 'the Bridge' so that Gina could book her on the Tour. But I wished to bid Emily goodbye. Though her personality was unsociable, and she ignored what was due to others in her circle, her honesty and forthrightness were appealing to me. There is something sad about a person who is so stubbornly attached to her own home that she cannot thrive outside of it. She cannot afford to lose another ounce of weight, and it is good she is to return.

Before I retired to bed, I went to her room and knocked. She was sitting up, playing with the scrawny kitten upon her lap. I think she was pleased that I had remembered her, and I said my goodbyes, and that was the end of it with Miss Emily Brontë. A genius? I have not read her *Wuthering Heights,* and if it is to come out in 1847, I shall be over seventy. I hope I will still have my sight to read, but we have nieces and nephews enough to read to us in our old age!

In the morning, we expect a sweeter addition to our party.

Yrs with great affection, Jane

Dear Cass

You are very bad not to write to me; I shall not forgive you until eleven o'clock.

Miss Anne Brontë is all Charlotte promised. She is very likable, wishes to please, and has a sweet smile. She is quite overcome with all that has become commonplace to us in just a week, is frightened of the noise, hates the hum, cannot bear the Hoover, etc. I learned that Miss Brontë had the wisdom to introduce young Lisa to the kitten, and made them fall in love with each other, so that now Lisa is engaged in a vigourous campaign with her mother to allow her to keep it.

Miss Anne was not the only visitor today. Ever before she emerged from upstairs, another arrived, also from afar, and by a means that seems impossible to me.

I rose early, as is my habit, and went to the parlour to play a few airs, and had just begun *Robin Adair* when the doorbell rang. It took me a moment to remember that anybody may answer a bell, and since I was the only one up, it fell to me.

I opened it to find a tall young man outside in greatcoat and fine woolen cravat – fair hair, blue eyes, a rather stern expression. I recognized him as Mr. Rowland Hatton from New York. Beside him was a younger woman, wrapped up warmly against the early morning air. My heart filled with anxiety. Who was this? What was this? Had Mr. Hatton married, and brought his bride to Ireland, and was now calling callously upon poor Gina?

'Um- good morning. I was told that Gina Romano is staying here,' he mumbled.

'She is – please come in,' I said, and I ushered him into the front parlour. I went upstairs to call Gina, my heart beating fast. I could not tell her who I thought the visitor to be, and my heart filled with dread for her. Then I put my head in to Maria, and shared the news with not a little consternation. Then I sped downstairs again, for I was hostess of the house until somebody else came along, and I felt very proud of myself in the business.

He was sitting uncomfortably on the chair next to the fireplace, and the woman was perched upon the sofa. But she was not his wife – or lover – the distance between them told me that. I began to hope.

I seated myself opposite him and began to be hostess.

'Permit me to introduce myself,' I said. 'I am Jane.'

'Jane,' he said. 'Do you live here, Jane?'

I was impressed that I could pass so easily for a modern person.

'No, I am a guest,' I said.

'You are one of Gina's Time Travel clients?'

'Yes. I have come from 1816 England.'

110

'How fascinating!' said the girl, and I realized she was younger than I thought. About seventeen. Was it – ?

This made Mr. Hatton remember his manners, and he then introduced himself as the man I already knew him to be, and presented his sister, Katy.

He grew quiet again, the picture of anxiety. I realized the stern expression was more apprehension than ill-humour. How I longed to set him at ease! But his agony, I knew, would not last long.

'You are up early this morning, Mr. Hatton.' I said conversationally. Somehow he was every inch a 'Mr.'

'We flew in at six, and came directly from Shannon Airport.' he said.

'What, you flew in the air?' My astonishment showed. 'In one of those – loud silver tubes?'

Katy laughed.

'Of course, being from 1816, that would be really weird,' she said. 'Are you a famous person, Jane?'

'I am – well-known in literary circles. I write novels.'

'What novels?' she asked, her eyes bright.

'*Pride and Prejudice* is one of them, *Sense and Sensibility* is another...'

Cassandra! Are you listening carefully? As soon as I opened my mouth, the reaction from both parties was Electrified. They sat up abruptly, opened their mouths wide, and cried: '*Pride and Prejudice*! But you're Jane Austen!'

'*Pride and Prejudice* is my favourite book!' Katy cried. 'And I just adore the Adaptations! The 1995 one with Colin Firth is superb! Mom and I watch it together every Christmas! Mr. Bennett is too funny! My Aunt Lucy prefers *Sense and Sensibility*. I watch the 2008 Adaptation with her at Easter. Dan Stevens is too cute as Edward - Oh! Jane Austen! I have to tell Mom I am talking to Jane Austen!' She whipped out her phone.

Her brother laughed and told her to wait; that Mom wouldn't understand yet about Gina's profession, and would think she was crazy, and it was 3am in New York. When Mr. Hatton – Rowland I ought to say – laughed, his face became softened; his eyes mirthful, and I could see his affectionate nature as he gently teased his young sister.

Then Gina appeared in her dressing-gown – a *robe* she calls it - looking wide-eyed, without cosmetics – her hair back in a pony - very taken aback as I was by the sight of the girl, until Mr. Hatton hurriedly introduced her, and I was just in time to hear him say: 'I brought her over so that she could meet you, Gina. She very much wanted to meet you,' before I reluctantly left them all to themselves.

So Cassandra, I have a great deal to think about until breakfast. Adaptations, Colin Firth, 1995, 2008, Too Cute, and Too Funny.

Later: Gina and her friends disappeared even before breakfast. Doug came in at ten, and was very angry to find her gone, and Mary, not knowing the true state of things, told him that 'Gina's boyfriend had come from America this morning with his sister, and they were all gone for the day.'

I no longer think anything good of Doug Shaw. He is greedy, self-serving, and mean-spirited. He told us to prepare our Speeches, and to keep it to 'twenty minutes max'. Mr. Thackeray was quite annoyed at this restriction, and Doug told him, cruelly, that only a handful of people in Limerick had ever heard of his *'Irish Sketches'*.

I have one more event of importance to relate to you, Cassandra. Shortly after nuncheon, I was alone in the parlour for a few minutes, and Eric came in with the laptop, and said: 'Jane! I forgot all about it! Let's do it now!' he set the laptop down. 'What did you want me to search for?'

I told him, inwardly steeling myself for results I would not be happy with. Eric's fingers tripped over the keys.

'Pride...and...Prejudice' We waited while the computer did whatever it is that computers do.

'Forty-five million five hundred thousand hits on 'Pride and Prejudice'.' he said.

'That is impossible!' I cried. 'It cannot be my book *Pride and Prejudice!'*

'There's only one. *Pride and Prejudice* by Jane Austen, first published 1813. 'Look for yourself!' He swiveled the machine over to my view.

Scanning the screen, my heart filled with a violent emotion which Miss Brontë, if she could but know of it, would greatly commend; I struggled greatly to become the mistress of myself, and not treat my host to a burst of tears.

'What about your other works?' Eric asked, with eagerness. I prompted him as to *Sense and Sensibility*, *Mansfield Park*, and *Emma* - he entered them in a blur of speedy fat fingers, and they all had an astonishing number of results, but P&P by far holds the most interest.

I refused to believe that I am more popular than Maria
Edgeworth. But I was too overcome to ask him to search for her
works – and I would not like to in any case - so I thanked him and
fled to the sanctuary of my room, and to the packets of tissue
handkerchiefs of which I have a good supply. Now I am very
affrighted indeed. I must stop - Yrs, Jane

Thursday September 29th

Dear Cassandra

You will think I have been in a dead faint for the last two days,
but after I had a little weep in my room, I washed my face and
resumed my place in company, and mentioned not a word of
what I found. I am still astonished and affrighted, though slowly
getting used to the grandeur of being renowned. But *why* so much
attention? That is the peculiar thing. I cannot be any more skilled
than others upon this tour. Much may be luck of course – who
read my work, and when, and who may have promoted it –and
what may have been the fashion - I truly am at sea.

Electric light is a blessing and a curse – it makes Day of Darkness.
It is now 3am. An hour ago, I took my cue from Emily Brontë and
stole downstairs to use Eric's laptop. I have observed how he
brought up Google, and how he placed the little flashing 'I' (none
of this makes sense to you, I know) in the box, and then keyed in
the letters, and pressed a key named 'Enter.'

I was very curious about Maria. I entered 'Belinda' but I got a
Singer, an Author, and a Gourmet Confectioner with a small cake
and a big smile, and I realized I would have to be more specific, so
I added Maria Edgeworth after it, and it 'came up' – 78,000 results
. I was disappointed; for I consider my judgment to be very good,

114

and am vexed she has not endured as well as I. 'Camilla' brought up a chirpy fairhaired lady who is married to Charles Prince of Wales; I wished to read all about present Royalty, but Time is of the essence in a secret nocturnal adventure, so I quickly found 'Fanny Burney's Camilla' the results are about the same as Maria's.

Still in the throes of terror about my own success, I hastily entered *Hamlet*. Relief at last! Hamlet is at least twice as admired as *Pride and Prejudice!*

What a relief to be less popular than Shakespeare. If my fellow-authors come to murder me in the night, I will mention it, and we can all go and hunt him down.

I must sleep. There is so much to be done in preparing our Speeches, and I confess to being very nervous about it.

Yours Affectly, JA

October 2nd 2016

Dear Cassandra

I had not much time to contemplate the subject last written of; we have had a great flurry of Activity; the rest of the week went very fast, and we had so much to arrange and accomplish. Saturday has come and gone; it was very gratifying, held great happiness for me in every way but one – and that one does not signify, because I will not allow it to dwell with me. Promise me you will not think of it either. But before I tell you about this, we have been taken to a Publick House by Gina and Rowland – Gina persuaded us – we went to The White House in George's – O'Connell St, (in Limerick since 1812!) and we assumed there would be a Snug for Ladies – there was none such – the Ladies sat in company with the Men. It was just as well, for there was Music. Though loud to our ears, it was enjoyable, for there were Ballads, and some of the melodies were familiar! You can depend upon it that any good thing will go on and on…

Before I begin, we are to prepare to return soon. I am only in a dilemma as to how much to give Anna, and I wish to buy a gift for Mary. And Gina of course.

At last Maria has found out the name of the Family who was most prominent in Limerick in the 19th century, but they are gone for the last one hundred years. Her clue was in the names of some Limerick streets, the impressive vaults seen in St. Mary's Cathedral, and the name of a Hospital, Barrington's. The family of that name lived some miles away in a place now called Glenstal Abbey near the village of Murroe. Of course we had to ask to be taken there – the drive, about 20 miles (30 minutes!), was very pleasant, with a great deal of country and woodland. The Abbey could well be Northanger, and if they were to set an 'Adaptation' here, I would be well satisfied, for it is a very grand house of red sandstone in an even grander, extensive park, and is now owned by Benedictine Monks, very civil, courteous men, who would surely disappoint Mrs. Radcliffe. We could not tour the house, but we did not miss any pleasure, as it is now a school for boys, and would not like to see what was once admirable (I am picking up Maria's word!) now plain and commonplace. We walked about the pretty glen and the gardens, for the Monks keep it in great order, and the trees are a lush and wondrous sight in all their red and gold beauty.

I forgot to enquire the whereabouts of Downton Abbey, but no matter.

But to the Re-Enacting Event! We had much to do; for we needed cloathes; and wished to obtain some stuff to make gowns etc, but Doug said there was no necessity for that trouble, and he had already ordered Period Costumes from a Theatrical Company. There was tremendous excitement when they arrived, Gina was present, and the Brontës room, which had a long glass, quickly became a dressing room as we tried them on. But then consternation – nothing fitted properly; we again demanded needles and thread, and having none of the right shades, we all walked out to Hickey's in Cruises' St, bearing scraps. We then turned the front parlour into a Mantua-Maker's as scissors and needles flew, taking in waists; taking up hems; strengthening seams; for these were Theatrical cloathes and not expected to be perfectly made, and had been well-worn and looked so. Maria had to cover a wine-stain with a rose of ivory silk. Mary, seeing all the work we had to do, brought a 'Sewing Machine' to us but it looked very complicated indeed to learn to thread the bobbin in the short time we had available, and she remarked that in any case she had never seen people work stitches so fast and so beautifully. And she knew a place where we could obtain cheap 'court shoes' as she termed them, and a cobbler who could cover them with material to match our gowns. Stockings! Not to be got in real silk…but as Maria said with wisdom, who will know?

On Saturday, we were very busy, but that only served to distract us from our nervousness. We had worried about our hair, but Gina did not fail us. She up-ended one of her colourful bags and a variety of irons, brushes and combs clattered upon the dressing-table. She then sat us down in turn and styled our hair, curling forehead curls for Maria, making the prettiest little ringlets for Anne. She proposed some make-up 'for the cameras' and as we were her prisoners, we consented to a little foundation, but no eye shadow, only a little rouge, and the merest touch of carmine upon the lips.

But now to describe our Dress! Maria's and my habits were outdated by at least *twenty* years, but I was content; for my gown was of a style that I wore as a young woman, and it made me feel twenty again! It was a white tamboured muslin gown with a coquelicot satin sash and scallops at the hem, trimmed also in coquelicot. Over it, I wore a fine Indian shawl of white cashmere with a long fringe. Maria's gown is rose and ivory; she has a sizeable train. We all have jewellery too – not real, Costume – but realistic enough. Reticules we had to fashion for ourselves, but they were never meant to carry Lecture Notes, and we fairly stuffed them in.

Doug had balked at providing Hats but we refused to appear without some head decoration and long gloves - so I ended up with a head decoration worn by an actress who played Emma in an Adaptation. I was Queen of Highbury! Maria wore tall ostrich feathers which added six inches to her height. The Brontës were splendidly attired; their gowns in the style I described them when I first saw them; with narrow waists and hooped skirts, but these are very frilly and flouncy. The sleeves are short and full. Oh, the colours - Cerise for Charlotte; Violet for Anne. Anne looked beautiful, but then we were all very ton, and only despaired of a Grand Ball to attend after the Event, with all the Mr. Darcys and Rochesters you could find to dance waltzes with. I said as much to Miss Brontë, but she said:

'Oh, Jane' (we are on first names now, since I pinned up her hem) '*I* would never be handsome enough to tempt Mr. Darcy!' I replied: 'But you know, Mr. Darcy says that only of the ladies he *really* means to dance with!'

Mr. Thackeray was pacing in the parlour, practicing his Speech, (we ladies had practiced them upon each other in the preceding days) and we proceeded down the stairs as if to a Grand Hall, but having gained the parlour, Gina suddenly turned, embraced us all and bid us goodbye. She too was dressed with care, in her long black silky dress with the lilac overlay; silver jewellery; a sparkling barrette in her hair, and we had assumed she would be with us for the night, indeed, we could not see how we could do without her. We were very taken aback, and she told us, haltingly, that she was not going to the Event, but that she would try to 'drop by' later. She assured us that we would 'do great' and we'd 'rock the house'. We were very disappointed, but her eyes were bright, and we could not but be happy for her, for we knew she must be meeting Rowland.

The Event – named *'Living History - 19th Century Authors'* was held in the University of Limerick's Concert Hall, and packed with attendees who paid quite a sum for Seats. I have never visited a place of august learning in my life and felt all the dignity of the occasion. Upon entering the Hall, I and my fellow authors were conducted to a table upon the stage, and were introduced in turn. Looking upon row upon row of eyes in the endless tiered seats, our stomachs filled with butterflies. A podium to our left was equipped with a 'microphone' - a device to make our voices louder.

Doug and Rena were there; Doug's job it was to adjust the microphone to our particular heights, and what a piece of work he made of it when it came to my turn. I spoke after Maria, and she being petite and I taller, it became necessary to adjust it...I was not aware of that necessity, and after I had said 'I bid you all a Good Evening!' and evidently nobody heard me except the people

119

in the front row, he trod over to jerk it upwards. I saw a little anger in his gesture. I felt a little foolish.

The approbation of the audience was a composing factor for me, and after pronouncing the first few sentences, I found I could speak freely indeed, and felt almost as happy as in the parlour at Steventon, when our whole family was in attendance as I read my works. I had been instructed to give my opinion as to why *Pride and Prejudice* has worn its years so well. Having thought about it extensively over the last few days, I decided that it's endurance is due to Elizabeth's personality, and how she was not to be intimidated by Rank or Riches, and how all young ladies would love to be like her. And then there is Mr. Darcy, rich, handsome, and of sound character. Every young woman dreams of Mr. Darcy. All of this was done very well, and I thought myself thoroughly the polished speaker, and only regretted that I could not do the same in the Hall at Alton![10]

During the course of the evening, after the first half-hour of questions or so, it became clear that the Audience were willing to believe us more and more to be our Real Selves rather than Re-enactors. Our authenticity, gestures and demeanor in general, our bewildered countenances when modern words were used and the necessity for Doug or Rena (who chaired the event) to interpret, suspended credibility in such a manner that many of the hearers entered completely into the spirit of Re-enacting, as they believed it to be.

The questions put to us were answered very competently – and some were very odd, such as:

---

[10] The town closest to Chawton Village.

'Miss Austen, I visited your house at Chawton, and saw the table you wrote on. How did you produce such great works on such a small table?'

And an obvious question for the Brontës:

'I don't see Emily Brontë here. Why only two of the famous Brontë sisters?'

Why indeed! Charlotte answered: 'Our sister Emily would not be seen on a publick stage such as this. She dislikes company. It would be very out of character, and we cannot be out of character.'

Later, as we 'mingled' among the crowd in the atrium, drinks in our hands, Maria came to me, and said, in a rather humble way: 'Jane, what I have heard tonight is that you and your works have given joy to many generations of people. An old dear told me that when she is lonely for her sisters, all deceased now, she watches 'Pride & Prejudice' on her DVD machine, and is again part of a lively family of girls.'

My work comforts those who mourn! Indeed it does not occur to me when I am writing, to 'console' the reader. Astonishing.

'But *this* I wish to tell you' Maria went on, almost breathless - 'a Prime Minister – name of Mr. Churchill - defending England from – a madman – a Prussian *I think* – very aggressive –! wished to take over the world –! this in the twentieth century – a horrible war! *Mr. Churchill* was ordered by his doctors to rest, and he had *Pride & Prejudice* read to him while he was recuperating. He returned to work invigorated and ready to lead England on to Victory – the Americans sailed to aid us – I had the entire History from that gentleman over yonder!'

Looking 'yonder' I saw the scholarly gentleman who had put me right upon the whereabouts of Georges St. He lifted his glass to me in recognition.

'Your work is very good Medicine, Jane!' Maria finished.

I doubt very much if *Pride & Prejudice* helped to save the world from the Prussian madman; it might just as well have been a work by Maria Edgeworth that the great Mr. Churchill had to hand. No doubt he also had at his disposal a competent physician, a good map, and stout Generals. But I thought it generous of Maria to give me this warm approbation, because she did not get many questions directed to her. But can you believe the Americans helping England in her time of need? – admirably done indeed. Who would have thought it? We are all friends now.

I did hear something of Maria, but we are not to divulge the future to our fellows, and so Maria must endure any disappointment she feels without knowing how she is celebrated. Eric told me that Maria would be remembered not only for her writing but also 'for all the hard work she did for the starving peasants during the Famine, and she was in her eighties at the time.' News of impending Famine was horrid indeed, and I dared not tell my friend.

A woman told me that she has a very 'fast-paced' life in Chicago, (America) and lives 28 floors up a building. (How does one live so high up? How unnatural! I feel very sorry for her). She told me that sometimes for her leisure, she takes her walk with Anne Elliot, Captain Wentworth and the Musgroves across the fields towards Winthrop. Bless me! A very commonplace country walk designed to bring the characters together and further the plot, and the nettles and nuts are what satisfies her – it struck me then that future generations find in old works a more leisured pace; a way

122

of life that may be more difficult now to find, a place to walk out and obtain fresh air.

However, the enduring love stories in the novels are what have the most appeal, for love will never go out of fashion. I heard all of this as well...and that the stories are 'a clean read, no sex or violence' – I have seen enough to disgust me to know what that means.

Forgive me, Cassandra, for this excess of self-congratulation, but I heard also that my characters are very life-like, and that the reader hates to close the book on them, and that gives rise to many of the Sequels! The Darcys live on in many forms; even in a murder mystery where poor Denny gets shot and Wickham is almost hanged for it. That amused me greatly.

Towards the end of the evening, Gina arrived. She made her way through the crowd to come straight to me, and with the happiest of looks told me that she and Rowland were engaged. I congratulated her warmly; and wished her the happiest of marriages.

'You were so right, Jane!' she whispered in my ear so fast I could hardly keep up with her words. 'Rowland was very hurt when I broke up with him and the way I did it was horrible. I really regret that now. He *was* preparing his mother for our meeting, for she did not wish him to marry until he was at least twenty-seven and established in a business. But she is now very accepting that he has to lead his own life. When Rowland heard that Doug and I were together, he realized I was not really to blame at all – he knows Doug is very skilled at getting people to believe what he wants them to believe.

'Katy really looks up to me as a big sister already. She's passionate about History, and Rowland is thinking of setting up a Time

123

Travel Company, and if he does, I would be involved of course - Jane! I have to find a job between now and then – 'cos I quit TTT today - but I'm sure I'll get something. I can flip burgers at McDonalds. But if we form our Company, will you be our first client? Oh please say yes! We have to get you to the Big Apple! New York! Limerick is pretty but so, oh so *quiet.*'

Limerick quiet! How much noisier was it possible for New York to be? I agreed, but told her to come back to me in the year 1795 or so, when I was *young.* I would tolerate the noise and bustle so much better and if New York is busier than Limerick, I would like to have youth on my side. I was just about to tell her that I would never, ever get into an Elevator again, but we were interrupted.

 Doug charged out of the crowd, angry.

'Gina, where have you been?' he asked her savagely. 'You were supposed be here. I had to do everything! Oh, and I heard about Hatton. You're making a huge mistake. Do you know that I could get you fired for your unexcused absence?'

'That sounds good to me, except I quit already. I don't work for TTT since 9am this morning. That's why Rena's here. Didn't she tell you? Oh, she is to replace me to take the Guests back tonight.'

Tonight! I am just getting to know how famous I am, and I have to go away!

'If you don't work for TTT and you didn't pay the entrance fee, *you* have no right to be here, so just leave.' Doug said.

'Gina is my guest,' I said quickly, assuming a role of self-importance and bestowing upon myself the right to have one hundred such if necessary. 'She may stay just as long as she wishes.' Doug turned away and stormed back into the crowd.

'That's kind of you, Jane, but Rowland and Katy are waiting in the car, Katy didn't want to come in –Doug hit on her recently, and she got a crush on him. Rowland was furious and Doug demanded money to leave Katy alone - at that, she – *and her Mom* - saw the light, thank God – Doug is out of Mrs. Hatton's life forever. Oh, Katy so needs a big sister! Now we're all going to Milano's for an Italian dinner. I have to go, oh Jane, thanks so much! I don't have any Aunts - I wish you could be my Aunt!'

'I have had a great deal of practice these twenty-three years,' I said to her, startled as she threw her arms about me and hugged me tightly. These times are different as I said, or is this the American way of showing regard? I rather regret my strong and unpleasant feelings about that country. Perhaps this newfound tenderness for the New World will still be with me when I wake.

Doug *hit on* Katy. If I were to stay any longer, I could write in a contemporary style. Imagine Mr. Darcy telling Elizabeth: *'Mr. Wickham hit on my kid sister'*. No, it would never do…

 I am sure that Doug knew I had advised against him, rather than for. And in his anger, he decided to punish me. A little while later, a man sidled up to me. He had sly eyes.

 'Miss Austen, do you know that the Park on which this University is built, was once owned by Lord Clive of India? He called it Plassey, after the Battle.'

'No, I did not! How interesting!' I halted, surprised – Lord Clive of India! He knew my Aunt and Uncle Hancock there.

'Are you familiar with the letter that Lord Clive wrote to his wife telling her to keep away from your Aunt Mrs. Hancock, because she had 'thrown herself into the power of Warren Hastings?'

Cassandra, I was shocked! I am sure the blood drained from my face, and I was barely able to speak, but when I did, I blurted:

'No – I have not heard of any such! I do not believe there is any such letter!'

'I can assure you that it exists and has been studied, and it is a genuine letter.'

Doug was hovering by; he was watching my great discomfort. But what happened next gave me great pain indeed.

He joined us, and said: 'Your cousin, Jane! Your beloved cousin Eliza de Feuillide, neé Hancock, was rumoured to be the daughter of the Governor of India, Warren Hastings.'

This was a scandalous allegation, and I felt all the distress of it, and all the shame that this rumour must do to our family, were it ever to spread in our own Times. That Govornor Hastings was Eliza's very generous *Godfather* we knew well. Eliza, our dear cousin, our beloved friend and sister, she at least would never have heard it, or felt the pain of it.

'Eight years childless, the Hancocks move to Bengal, party hard with Warren Hastings, and hey! Mrs. Hancock is pregnant!' Doug said.

'Mr. Shaw, you are no gentleman.' I said to him.

'Your Aunt Hancock was no lady,' he said.

'Doug?' said a voice behind him. I saw Rena.

She took him aside and dismissed him! He pleaded to no avail – she told him to report to TTT Headquarters for his Exit Interview in two days, where he would receive the pay due to him – and if he ever came to TTT Headquarters after that, Security would eject

126

him. He was to hand over his ID Badge to her *now*. (I understand it contains access to all of TTT's computer programs). He was to travel economy to New York on a commercial flight. He again tried to plead, to charm, to explain away – it was all meant as a joke – he threw me a look as if to support him in this particular defense - but Rena had seen and heard enough. She had been summoned by somebody who saw that Doug intended harm to me - but who had that been? I saw Miss Brontë by – had it been Charlotte?

And Doug Shaw at last conceded defeat, and walked away, but he had left me in a very unpleasant state of mind.

So, dear Cass, Fame and Success are not free! Oh, Cass, if it was true, it must have been some extraordinary circumstance that caused our Aunt to act so. Our Uncle Hancock treated Eliza as his own darling daughter. She was his only child. But she was so unlike him, in her charming and happy nature! She did not inherit her liveliness from Aunt Hancock either. Governor Hastings had an affectionate nature and an engaging personality…wherever Eliza came from, she was an enchanting creature and loved all of us, as we did her.

Rena apologized to me for Doug's behavior with great profusion. But the rumour is there in History. But am I the cause of its being publick? Warren Hastings must be a person of greater renown than I could ever be. A Governor, a Member of the Privy Council. I hope it is from his biographers that the rumour stems. But to return to my Drama - Rena then hurried after Gina to offer her Doug's position! So she will not have to 'flip burgers' in McDonalds, which by the way, we have visited, Gina saying it was an essential part of modern experience. It has no appeal for me, being without beauty or elegance - it was very bright with yellows and greens, and full of children. The furniture is bolted to

127

the floor. No tableware of any kind; and hardly a knife or fork, and those very thin and 'plastick' – a pliable material, easily broken. However, McDonalds is very popular and is found all over the world, so why should you listen to me.

But now I shall have to end, but not before I heard something very happy just as the Atrium was emptying and the tables became full of empty glasses, used plates and crumpled napkins, testimony of an evening well-spent.

A very nice lady came to me, and told me the following: I shall put it quite simply – that Tom Lefroy, in answer to a question by his nephew, admitted later in life that he had been in love with me. Though it was, he had said, 'a boyish love.'

But he would say that; would it not be offensive to his deceased wife and their children to say otherwise? And yet I hope he was happy with his wife, and their letters to each other, portions of which I have seen in his memoirs in the Granary-Library, (I went there again, and marched everybody to the Barnful of Books) are very affectionate. He was very fond of his wife, as all husbands should be, and was a good family man.

But I was gratified to hear of his admission because I knew that he had felt as I had. O but not at all surprised…and furthermore, I was told that the only reason Tom Lefroy is remembered at all is because of the Christmas he spent at Steventon with his Aunt. Astonishing for the Lord Chief Justice of Ireland to be remembered chiefly as the partner of Miss Jane Austen at our humble assemblies!

Other sensations crowded in upon me in the course of the even, as I learned much of how – famous – I am now. (If I lived to the age of 240, I would be very, very Rich). I am in hopes that I will realize some riches in my lifetime. I can help so many people. You, our mother, our friends, *Henry* without whose help none of this could have been, as he paid for the publishing of *Sense and Sensibility*!

I have known the ecstasy of receiving payment for my labours, labours of love - but I am confounded by the Industry Jane Austen became in the late twentieth century and beyond - the Austenesques, the Portrayals (that was Mr. & Mrs. Darcy on the Mug) the Jane Austen Center in Bath, Scholarly Papers, Theses, *Janeites*, my oak-leafed Pelisse on display at Hampshire museum, more than one Biography - *My Head upon the 10-Pound Note!*

No, it is too much; it affrights me greatly; it is far beyond anything – almost like idolatry - am ready to come back – if I stay any longer I am afraid I shall worship myself.

Cassandra, do not be uneasy. You shall not have to deal with a sister with an Unbearable Conceit when we shall wake. It will just be another commonplace morning – I will get up, say my Morning Prayer, dress and go downstairs to play a jig, then make the toast for you, our Mother, and Martha. I shall simply be Miss Jane Austen of Chawton Cottage, and later I will take my Quill and dip it in the ink, and create characters that endure to give Joy to a very different world, without my being aware of one bit of it.

 God - the Giver of all gifts – does He guide my hand?

Your Loving Sister
Jane

THE END

'PERSUASION' CHARACTERS SPEAK OUT!

or *'The Elliot Pride'*

Sir Walter Elliot, Baronet, of Kellynch Hall.

At first, when I heard that my daughter Anne was the centre of a story - a long story - about her hankering after Captain Wentworth - now my son-in-law, I need hardly say - I was quite annoyed and deplored the state to which we have descended nowadays, when the intimacies of a gentleman's family should be known to all and sundry. I had no intention of reading the work.

However, it gained some popularity among my Lords in the House, because I began to be noticed even more than heretofore, and greeted with distinction in the lobby of the House of Commons, and one day, a fellow who I habitually avoid because of a particularly ugly wart on his chin which I cannot bear to look at, and eyebrows brushes of harsh brown straw, came straight to me with this publication in his hand, and making a sweeping bow, declared that it did me great credit indeed, and opening the work with a flourish to the first page of Chapter 1, he pointed his short and stubby finger to my name and I saw that it was I, Sir Walter Elliot, led off the story, followed by the description of our family in the Baronetage.

My lawyer and agent Mr. Shepherd has made me see that this is indeed a compliment to my Nobility and Rank, to be portrayed thus, in all importance and with the awareness of that importance. So, I bade him obtain 'Persuasion' and mark all the references to myself. I am not at all interested in how Anne got Captain Wentworth, and the doings and caprices of the Misses Musgroves are not worthy of my notice.

'He had been remarkably handsome man in his youth; and, at fifty-four, was still a very fine man' - that is pleasing enough, though a longer and clearer description of my looks would have not gone astray — tall person, blue eyes, cleft chin; I could go on. Ah! Now I object to the notion of retrenching, as any gentleman should. My description of the

seafaring men is very amusing indeed, and I am gratified that the points of objection that I have to the Navy, that of raising men of obscure birth into undue distinction, is related in full. I hope that is taken note of and that the Lords of the Admiralty will be influenced to become more select in choosing who to promote to elevated ranks. My observation that sailors lose their looks in a rapid time under all weathers may be noted as well, but as that is hardly a matter for England's safety, it may be passed by, as it is to be supposed that the French sailor has his looks cut up in equal measure. Indeed it would not do if the French sailors surpassed our own men in good looks. Therefore, I may wish them a bigger navy but only for more of them to be blown about.

Ah! The Author – one Miss Austen of no name whatsoever, a clergyman's daughter – I should be ashamed if my daughters wrote a novel – but no matter – she now places me in Bath. This is most pleasing; 'a very good house in Camden Place, a lofty dignified situation'. Whatever my quibbles about clergymen's daughters writing novels, this girl is capable of housing families of consequence, and my vociferous objection to my daughter visiting a Mrs. Smith in some low part of town are well documented. She gives a good enough account of the Elliot connections when she mentions the Dowager Viscountess Dalrymple and her attentions to me.

But allow me make it apparent now, and forevermore, that I never, ever had any intention of marrying Mrs. Clay. A woman of low birth; fit only to be a companion, which is little more than an upper servant! The fears of my family (excepting Elizabeth, who knows me the best) are exaggerated. Do they know me so little as to suppose I would degrade myself thus? If I should think of marrying again, I would consider Lady Dalrymple's daughter the Honourable Miss Carteret, though I have been afforded one glimpse of her ancles, and they are not at all pretty – but it is always to be hoped that next year's fashions will have gowns long enough to cover such monstrosities.

In all I am very pleased with my portrayal, and should anyone else wish to write about me, I am at leisure to make them conversant with the Barony of Kellynch and the Elliot family.

Mary Elliot Musgrove, youngest daughter of the Baronet

Dear Readers,

I am Mary Elliot Musgove, wife of Charles, and I am one of the main characters in Jane Austen's novel, 'Persuasion'.

I am writing this letter in great indignation, because of the inaccurate portrayal of myself, Anne's sister, in the book. I am perfectly aware that the story is about Anne, and that therefore she takes centre stage, (though goodness knows why Anne's story should be any more interesting than mine) but that is the way Austen created her book, and in order to make Anne look more interesting, she makes her sisters - indeed her entire family - look unreasonable, vain, sharp, unpleasant, and at times, almost comical.

I wish to offer my sincere objection to Austen's portrayal of myself as a cross, nagging, ill-humoured wife.

But what I find most objectionable is the allegation that it was Anne, not I, Mary, who was Charles' Musgrove's *first* choice of wife, and that it was only after being refused by Anne that he turned his attentions to me. That rankled above everything else of annoyance in the novel. What if the world should believe it? I took it to be a blatant lie, made up by Louisa Musgrove to further her intimacy with Captain Wentworth by appearing to 'let him in on' the intimate affairs of her family. (The Musgrove girls are very forward). However, upon complaining to my husband Charles about Louisa, and asking him to speak to her about it, and to demand that she write forthwith to apologise to me, he admitted Louisa's statement to be true - however he explained it in a manner satisfactory to me, which I shall now relate to you.

135

Charles explained that he had *always* preferred me to my sisters. I am without a doubt that I was the prettiest and the most lively in manners and conversation, and he agreed with me when I reminded him of it. Bear in mind, however, that I am the *youngest* daughter of Sir Walter Elliot. When the time came for him to marry, he felt keenly the offence offered to the older Elliot sisters if the youngest should marry first. However, my sister Elizabeth, it was known, had her sights on nobility, far above anything that the Musgroves could ever aspire to. So he proposed to Anne, who was next. He knew she would refuse him, and when she did so, as he expected, he was at last free to propose marriage to me, his favourite, having discharged his duty to my older sister.

This is a very satisfactory explanation, for I do not believe for a moment that Anne would be preferred to me! What were Anne's charms compared to mine? She is a good girl and makes herself useful, but dull - one never even notices if Anne is in the room!

There was one more point to be cleared up - what, I put it to Charles, if Anne had accepted him? He replied that he knew that Anne would not accept him because of the way in which he phrased his offer, indeed, he made it clear to Anne, he says, that his honour demanded that he ask her first, before me - he made it clear that I was his favourite - and put in such a way, she had no option *but* to refuse him.

So I hope it is clear now that Charles wanted me for his wife from the very outset, not Elizabeth, and not Anne. After we had this conversation, he took his gun out and killed a very great number of birds, and I hope, dear Reader, that you are now at ease about the situation, as I am. I do think that Miss Austen could have explained it more fully.

Mrs. Penelope Clay, daughter of the Baronet's Agent Mr. Shepherd, and companion to the eldest Miss Elliot.

Jane Austen is not fond of me, and I am sure the reader shares this view. I am some dreadful things - insinuating, cunning, very ready to supplant Miss Anne in the affections of her sister Elizabeth. But I shall not be blamed for the lack of affection in that quarter – that state of affairs existed long before Miss Elliot chose me to become her companion.

The author tells you that I made an 'unprosperous' marriage. I shall relate more of my history to you – painful as it is – shameful in parts. But I care not – I have found this world to be hard and unforgiving, and not everybody can afford the luxury of goodness.

I was seventeen when I met Robert Clay and was married to him before I was eighteen. (I had not the benefit of a Lady Russell to persuade me to refuse him). Robert was a sailor – an able seaman – though my father allowed our neighbours to think he was made - and he moved me to Plymouth. We had four children, of whom two survived.

Robert, when in port, spent most of his time in taverns. I often had to search the streets for him at night to find money for food, for if he did not come home, I would not be able to feed the children or myself. I often did not find him. But I found other men. They paid me money. A very degrading situation, but I was in the greatest wretchedness. It was a desperate time, and it made me become, later, all that you saw, in 'Persuasion'. I had to provide for myself and I vowed, after that period in my life was over, that I would never allow want in my or my childrens' lives again.

(Do you remember the only long speech I made in 'Persuasion'? It was in defence of the sailor, and I quietly relished the ignorance of the Elliot family in knowing the extent of my declared intimacy with the profession!)

Mr. Clay disappeared somewhere in the Pacific Islands. The Navy opined that he had gone back to a native woman, and was therefore a deserter. I received no money; but after a seven-year absence, I was entitled, by law, to call myself a Widow.

During this seven years, I had the fortune to become mistress to a Ship's Captain named John Quigley, who kept me in a modest apartment with a maid, and paid for my children to be sent away to school. My family never suspected, as there was never a visit from anybody from that part of the country. I led them to believe I was companion to an elderly lady. After several years, my Captain gave in to the entreaties of his family and married the woman of their choice. Our leave-taking was pitiful indeed. We were fond of and understood each other, and had a child – a girl. She was three years old and sent away to a school. If I ever weep, it is for my little Jane.

After the Captain's marriage, I wrote to my father, Mr. Shepherd, stating that the old lady had died, and died poor, so that I was now in a bad situation. My children were taken out of school, (except Jane – my father was ignorant of her existence) and we went back to my father's house. I explained my smart dresses and bonnets by saying that Mrs. Smurfit's family had given them to me in place of the money owed to me in wages, and if they seemed a little bright and fashionable for the tastes of an old lady, he never noticed.

The gowns which Captain Quigley had supplied me with served me to great purpose on my visits to Kellynch Hall, which became frequent. I was of course acquainted with the family since childhood, and I and Miss Elizabeth, who was just a little younger than myself, had played together a few times. While I was never as elegant as Elizabeth, and was careful to observe the distinctions in rank, she was nevertheless pleased to see that I dressed with care and that I was fit for her drawing room and later, for the remove to Bath when she asked me to accompany her instead of her sister Anne. The statement: *'no-one will want Anne in Bath'* gratified me. I was Elizabeth's dearest friend now, her confidante, but I had bigger hopes – I intended one day to become her mother! And why not? Sir Walter Elliot was worth throwing my cap at. In spite of his obvious vanity, and his criticism of my freckles, for which he recommended various treatments, I knew how to make myself liked. He had been widowed many years; he was evidently pleased with me; and I was young enough to bear another child – a boy – his longed-for heir.

I had great hopes of Bath. But young Mr. Elliot, the prodigal cousin, arrived. He was heir. He suspected, from the first, my intention, and saw that if I was to marry Sir Walter, he could lose all intended for him. He wished to be rid of me. He allowed me to know that he had made some enquiries of me, and that made me very uneasy. I spent many nights thinking about my children and what exposure would do to them. They would have no expectation of a place in any society. The future looked very hopeless, unless – I secured young Mr. Elliot for myself. I had to contrive to become his mistress - I would not aspire to marriage – that I knew was a hopeless prospect. But I had been mistress before, and it would suffice until he tired of me. My existence is a very precarious one. It was wrong of me to become his mistress when he was expected to marry Miss Anne Elliot, but what do I care for her? What does she care for me? As for Elizabeth, who hoped to catch him for herself, I laugh up my sleeve about Elizabeth.

When I found out that Mr. Elliot was not to marry Miss Anne after all, my entire situation was thrown again into uncertainty. He quitted Bath for Town, and sent for me soon after, but before I left I contrived to find out something of my old society in Plymouth, from my acquaintance with Admiral Croft.

He and his wife are very pleasant people, and willing to talk without suspecting any motive in the person with whom they converse. I called upon them, to bid them goodbye. I turned the subject to the Navy, and mentioned men whom I inferred were my poor late husband's friends in Plymouth, and regretted that I had not heard anything of them for an age. There was Captain Goode and Lieutenant Ellis and Captain Quigley – I had not even a blush as the last name fell from my lips – but, having listened to Admiral Croft speak at great length of the first Captain's prize-money and the house he has built with it – and the professions and marriages of all of the children of the Lieutenant, he said something that was sweet music to my ears: *'poor Quigley's wife died, I heard, about a year ago.'*

Young Mr. Elliot will ensure his mistress is well adorned; I already have new gowns and jewels. After some weeks I shall leave him *for a month to see my husband's relations in Plymouth*. I shall see Captain Quigley to enquire after our child. I shall not appear to be in any need. I have Gowlans lotion – consistent use, as the Baronet advised, has improved my complexion.

Do you understand me a little better now, Reader? If you do not, I am sure I do not care at all.

The End

The Author is from Limerick, Ireland, and moved to the Pacific Northwest USA in 1995. That was the year of the BBC/A&E *Pride and Prejudice* Adaptation, and she has been a Janeite ever since. She is currently working on a Sequel to *Sense & Sensibility,* and has numerous other projects, big and little.

Visit Mary online at www.celticjaneite.net

the Facebook Page for *My Head upon the 10-Pound Note* is: https://www.facebook.com/myheadupon/

There may be more characters Speaking Out from Austen Novels in the future, as soon as they find the Courage.

www.ingramcontent.com/pod-product-compliance
Lightning Source LLC
Chambersburg PA
CBHW071308130626
46556CB00004B/1519